"Want to go swimming?" Dev asked.

No, no, no. The last thing she needed was to put herself anywhere near a half-naked man who already drove her crazy.

"Sure. I'll meet you there in a few minutes. I need to change." Was that voice hers? What happened to no?

"I'll wait."

"Oh. I'll just be a minute."

Slipping into the silken water a few moments later, Georgia threw caution to the wind. One more night couldn't hurt—she couldn't fall any more in love. When Dev reached for her, she moved into his arms with no hesitation. Encircling his neck, she kissed him with abandon, letting her love consume them both.

D0727973

Dear Reader,

Welcome to BEAUFORT BRIDES, a trilogy about three sisters who untangle a web of deceit from the past and discover that the solving of this puzzle leads to a gorgeous bridegroom and a glorious wedding for each of them!

My three heroines, Margot, Shelby and Georgia, are all very different, yet their qualities complement each other perfectly. Margot has a strong sense of responsibility, Shelby is quiet and shy and Georgia is outrageous and daring. I like to think that I have something of each of these women in myself!

I had a wonderful time developing stories for these remarkable sisters and the extraspecial men in their lives. Together they determine to follow their hearts until the truth about their father is revealed. I invite you to come and see....

Barbara McMahan

GEORGIA'S GROOM
Barbara McMahon

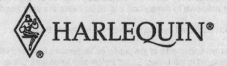

TORONTO • NEW YORK • LONDON
AMSTERDAM • PARIS • SYDNEY • HAMBURG
STOCKHOLM • ATHENS • TOKYO • MILAN • MADRID
PRAGUE • WARSAW • BUDAPEST • AUCKLAND

If you purchased this book without a cover you should be aware
that this book is stolen property. It was reported as "unsold and
destroyed" to the publisher, and neither the author nor the
publisher has received any payment for this "stripped book."

ISBN 0-373-03620-5

GEORGIA'S GROOM

First North American Publication 2000.

Copyright © 2000 by Barbara McMahon.

All rights reserved. Except for use in any review, the reproduction or
utilization of this work in whole or in part in any form by any electronic,
mechanical or other means, now known or hereafter invented, including
xerography, photocopying and recording, or in any information storage
or retrieval system, is forbidden without the written permission of the
publisher, Harlequin Enterprises Limited, 225 Duncan Mill Road,
Don Mills, Ontario, Canada M3B 3K9.

All characters in this book have no existence outside the imagination of
the author and have no relation whatsoever to anyone bearing the same
name or names. They are not even distantly inspired by any individual
known or unknown to the author, and all incidents are pure invention.

This edition published by arrangement with Harlequin Books S.A.

® and TM are trademarks of the publisher. Trademarks indicated with
® are registered in the United States Patent and Trademark Office, the
Canadian Trade Marks Office and in other countries.

Visit us at www.eHarlequin.com

Printed in U.S.A.

PROLOGUE

GEORGIA BEAUFORT breezed into the office like a woman on a mission. She had it all planned. She just needed to convince her two brothers-in-law. She'd been toying with the idea for more than a week and knew she had all her ducks in a row. Both were stubborn men, however, and if they said no, she'd have to go back to square one. But optimism was one of her strong traits and she had to hold on to the belief she'd get her way.

"Good morning," she said, trying to put as much confidence into her manner as possible as she greeted her sister Shelby's new husband. Patrick O'Shaunnessy was skilled at reading people. It came in handy in his business, that of a private investigator. She didn't want any of her doubts to surface as he'd hone in on them in an instant.

She still had trouble believing her sister Shelby had married him on such short acquaintance. But Shelby adored him, so for that alone, Georgia was happy to welcome him as part of the family.

"Patrick," Rand Marstall said in greeting, walking in behind Georgia.

Glancing at Rand, Georgia smiled confidently. She'd known him since he'd first married her oldest sister, Margot, six years ago. Totally comfortable around the business magnate, she was counting on him backing her up. He absolutely doted on her sister—especially now that Margot was pregnant. And after all, Margot had started this quest to find their father. Now Georgia could do something to bring it to an end.

Patrick stood and looked warily at the two people who had just invaded his office.

"Good morning, I think. To what do I owe this unexpected honor?"

Rand shrugged and glanced at Georgia. "I'm not sure. This meeting was her idea. And I'm under strict instructions to say nothing about it to Margot."

"Oh, oh. Sounds like Shelby's last scheme—and I ended up married to her!" Patrick said, motioning his visitors to sit. Sinking into his desk chair, he gazed at Georgia. "Something tells me I'm not going to like this."

"Ha, shows how much you know." Georgia pulled her chair close to the desk and pulled a folder from her carryall. Slapping it on the desk, she looked up expectantly.

"Recognize that?"

Patrick nodded slowly. "It's the office folder regarding your father's search. Shelby took it a few weeks ago."

"She left it at my place," Georgia confirmed. Flicking a glance at Rand, she turned back to Patrick. "You have a dossier for three men who match most of the facts we've compiled on Sam Williams. How long do you think it will take to visit each of these men and interview them? I, for one, am anxious to know if one is my father."

"These things take time, Georgia. This is not the only case my firm is working on, you know."

"Well, time's been passing ever since Grandmother trumped up that murder charge that drove our father away before I was even born! How much more time will it take?" Frustration bubbled up.

She had never known her father. Margot and Shelby each had fleeting memories, but she had none. All her life, she'd missed the family she should have had due to the machinations of her status-proud grandmother. Now that the dream of her life—meeting her father—was close, she was impatient to locate him.

Patrick glanced at Rand and then shrugged. "I know it's been more than twenty years since he was last seen, but Margot and Rand only discovered he hadn't left voluntarily a few months ago. With the scarcity of information, we've done well to identify these three men as possibles. These things take time."

"You've been on the case since mid-June. It's now the first week in August. How much time do you need? You already have all this information. Why can't we go confront each man and ask if he's our father? I want very much to locate him, you know that."

"I do know. And it'll only take a few more weeks. I need to travel to each location, arrange to speak privately with each man and go from there. If your father still thinks there's a murder charge hanging over him, I don't want to spook him by phoning first. Progress has been made—we've pretty much narrowed the field down to these three men. Can a few more weeks matter?"

"Maybe not to Margot or Shelby," Georgia said

restlessly. "Both obviously have other things on their minds with new husbands, new homes, new families. Which is as it should be. But I've just finished my last training course at the hospital and have some time on my hands."

She looked at Rand and then Patrick, smiling triumphantly. "I've thought of a way to speed up this step."

"And that is?" Rand asked cautiously.

"If we each take one suspect, and make a quick visit to each location, we can have the answer by the end of the week! Rand often flies to California for business, he could check out the man in Burbank and Margot would never guess what he's up to, or get her hopes up."

"I think she could handle it," Rand said dryly. "The doctor says she's healthy as can be. She is not going to miscarry this baby."

"Of course not. Still, we are all taking great care not to get her stressed or worried. I think if none of these men is our father, she would be hugely disappointed. Anyway, it doesn't hurt to keep it a secret until we know for sure.

"You, Patrick, can go to New Jersey. And I'll go to Houston and check out that one."

"Or we can wait a while—I'll take each in turn and have the answer then," Patrick said.

"But I don't want to wait! The timing is perfect right now. I have several weeks vacation due me before I start my new job at the hospital. I'll spend the first couple of days in Houston, talk to the man, and then I'll have the rest of the time to enjoy my vacation. You two know how much it means to me and my sisters to find our father.''

Rand leaned back in the visitor's chair and steepled his fingers. ''Actually, it's not a bad plan.''

''It's a great plan,'' Georgia said, turning to him in relief, glad Rand backed her up.

''It could work,'' Patrick added slowly.

Georgia beamed at him. ''Of course it'll work. Piece of cake. Then it's settled? I'll take the Houston Sam Williams. We can keep in touch by phone. This time next week, we'll know for sure if one of these three is our father!''

CHAPTER ONE

SLAMMING down the phone, Georgia jumped up and paced the small motel room, fuming. She couldn't believe the man! She'd been calm and rational. And he'd accused her of being some kind of fortune-hunting hussy! Ohhh! She clenched her fists, wanting to scream!

Storming over to the window, she slid it open and gazed out over the strip of grass that softened the stark environs of the motel. Taking a deep breath, she held it a moment before letting it whoosh out. Reviewing the conversation, she tried to see where it had gone wrong. What could she have done differently?

She'd asked for Samuel J. Williams, only to be told he was out of the office. Directed to the acting Executive Manager, Dev Tolliver, Georgia had been forthright and honest. She'd introduced herself and then explained she was trying to verify if Samuel Williams had lived in Mississippi about twenty-three years ago. If he had been married once to a woman named Beaufort?

Dev Tolliver had not been equally forthcoming. When he'd pressed her as to why she was calling, she had responded she thought she might be Sam Williams' daughter. The obnoxious man on the other end laughed shortly, then lambasted her. How had she discovered Sam was ill? Was that the reason for her obvious ploy of trying to worm her way into some money? Samuel Williams had never lived in Mississippi and if she called again, he'd inform the authorities!

Just hearing the echo of his tone ignited her anger. Slapping a hand against the wall beside the window, she whirled around and paced back to the phone. She wished she could set that arrogant individual back on his heels. She wanted nothing from her father but to discover who he was. Where he was living. That he was all right.

Talk to him to learn what he'd been doing during the last twenty-some years.

Sinking slowly on the bed, she hesitated. There was no proof that this man was her father. That was the entire reason for her presence in Houston—to discover the truth. The acting Executive Manager sounded certain the man had never lived in Mississippi. Would he know that?

Maybe Patrick or Rand had already discovered that one of the other men was her father.

She'd phone and find out before pursuing this further. But if neither of the others proved to be the man they were searching for, then Mr. Tolliver would soon learn that she wasn't easily pushed aside. Discovering the truth was too important to her. She would find a way!

Snatching up the phone, she punched in the number to Patrick's office and waited, frustration still roiling inside.

Six days later Georgia slipped the key into a lock and turned it. Opening the door, she peeked inside. With a quick, guilty glance over her shoulder, she lifted her suitcase and entered. The small apartment was hers. The guilt came from the way she'd obtained it.

Closing the door, she set her bag on the floor and went to the window to open the blinds. Sunlight flooded the room. Turning, she surveyed the living room.

Neat and austere, it waited only for someone to breathe life into it. The furniture was functional, and there were no pictures on the walls, no magazines or books. Nothing to give the room personality. It awaited its next tenant.

Which was her—temporarily.

She crossed to the phone. Pleased to find it connected, she quickly dialed. She carried it with her to stand by the window gazing over the estate while it rang on the other end. Shelby answered. Taking a deep breath, Georgia tried out a fake New York accent. Could it fool anyone who knew her?

"Shelby O'Shaunnessy?"

"Yes?"

"I'm trying to reach your husband, Patrick."

"I'm sorry, he's unavailable right now. May I take a message?"

"Ask him to call Georgia Brown."

"Georgia? Is that you?"

"Hi, Shelby. Yes, it's me," Georgia said in her normal tone, almost laughing.

"What in the world are you doing? I didn't recognize you at first."

"Good, that was the idea."

"What idea? Where are you? Still in Houston?"

"Yes. Actually, I'm at Sam Williams' home."

"At his house? You got through to him? Is he our father?"

"No. I've spent the best part of a week just trying to get some information about him, or trying to arrange an appointment with the acting Executive Manager—who refuses to have anything to do with me or my calls. Samuel Williams is out of the office sick. His secretary is like a bulldog and refuses to tell me anything. Nothing gets by her."

Georgia smiled smugly. "Well, almost nothing. I'm trying another way. Circumventing Dev Tolliver and the guardian secretary, if you must know."

"What does that mean? Who's Dev Tolliver?"

"Apparently *the* man in charge in Samuel Williams' absence. Some officer in the company with delusions of omnipotence. He won't even speak to me."

For a moment the frustration surfaced. Taking a deep breath, Georgia continued, "One day I went to the offices determined to get in to see somebody who could give me information, but there was a big meeting going on about some oil well crisis and rather than hang around all day, I left. In the elevator on the way out I overheard two secretaries talking about how hard it was proving to find a live-in gardener for the Williams' estate."

"You didn't!" Shelby exclaimed.

"Yep, I faked a résumé, applied and got the job."

"What? Georgia, you don't know anything about gardening. You're a nurse."

"How hard can it be to cut back a few flowers? Anyway, I only need to pretend for a day or so. It's the only way. When I originally tried to explain the situation to Mr. Tolliver on the phone, he immediately tagged me as a gold-digger—and threatened to call the authorities. Once I can get in to see Sam Williams, talk to him face-to-face, I'll have the answer and be on my way. But just in case they check references before I can get in to see him, I listed you. And I said I was Georgia Brown. And that I'm from New York. I can't take the chance Mr. Tolliver will recognize my voice if he's running interference here as well as at the office. So if they call to check, say I was the best gardener you ever had."

"I can't believe you! This is the craziest stunt I've heard. And why Georgia Brown?"

"I had to come up with something since I'd told the secretary that first day that I was Cecilia Beaufort."

"Cecilia? Why on earth did you give that name? I know it's your first name, but you never use it."

"It seemed like a good idea at the time. In case Mom and Dad ever discussed names for future children or something. I thought he might recognize it. For all we know, it could be his mother's name."

"Then he'd be expecting you to be Cecilia *Williams*."

"Oh, I guess you're right." Georgia waved her hand in the air as if brushing away a minor detail. "Anyway, if anyone calls, make sure to back me up on this. Have you heard anything more from Patrick or Rand?"

"I don't expect Patrick to call until later, but he did finally get an appointment with the man in New Jersey. Rand's guy is still out of town and won't be back until next week. Rand's not staying away from

Margot that long, so will have to make another trip to the West Coast.''

Georgia shook her head. ''Last week I thought for sure we'd know by now, and yet here we are with none of the suspects eliminated.''

Shelby laughed softly. ''Suspects, indeed. You make them sound like criminals. One could be our father!''

''Well, I don't know what else to call them. I'm not unpacking until I see if I can catch this Sam Williams today. I don't know how ill he is, but unless he's bedridden, maybe I can run into him right away. Don't you think he's sure to walk around the yard at some point?''

''Unpacking?''

''I get an apartment over the garage included as part of the package for the job.''

''Good grief. How in the world did you get hired?'' Shelby asked. Georgia could hear the incredulity in her sister's voice and smiled again.

''Well, I fudged a bit on the qualifications,'' Georgia said, delighting in the way things had turned out.

Her attention was drawn to the snazzy black sports car that pulled to a stop in front of the garage—powerful, with sleek lines. An expensive man's toy. The driver climbed out and looked around. He was tall, dark and gorgeous.

''Wow,'' she said softly.

''What?''

''You should see what just drove up. Oh my gosh, he's heading for the steps that lead up here. I've got to go.'' Hanging up, Georgia snatched her suitcase and stashed it in the bedroom. Two seconds later she heard the rap on the door.

Running her fingers through her short blond hair, she took a deep breath. Checking to make sure her suit was still tidy, she reached for the doorknob. If this was the owner of the estate, he definitely wasn't her missing father—too young by far.

She opened the door and almost stopped breathing. Tall, dark and gorgeous, all right—even half hidden behind the mirrored lenses of his sunglasses. He wore a dress shirt, opened at the throat, his tie loosened, and dark charcoal-gray slacks. The clothes couldn't camouflage the rugged width of his shoulders, nor his height—which had to be over six feet.

The dark glasses hid his expression. What color were his eyes? Dark and yummy like the rest of him, she bet, wishing he'd take them off.

"Georgia Brown?" he asked.

Her attention caught—her heart dropped. His voice was the one she'd heard over the phone when she'd first called the oil company's headquarters. Deep and husky, reminding her of sultry nights in the bayou. This was Dev Tolliver! What was he doing here?

She took a shaky breath, her heart racing. Would he recognize her voice despite her fake accent? Kick her out before she had a chance to locate and talk with Sam Williams? Call the authorities?

She nodded—answering to the name she'd used to obtain the position. Pure dumb luck got her here—but some fast thinking would be needed to stay!

"Yes."

"Dev Tolliver," he said, holding out his hand.

"Sorry I didn't get a chance to meet you at the office. My secretary, Janice, told me she'd hired you."

Georgia boldly placed her hand in his, almost snatching it back when an unexpected jolt of awareness shot up her arm. Eyes wide, she stared at him, her heart thundering in her chest. What did he want? Why had he come?

"I thought I was hired to work for a Samuel Williams," she said, trying the New York accent again. If she could fool Shelby for a few seconds, surely she could fool a man who had only spoken with her once briefly on the phone.

"That's right. Samuel's my stepfather." Dev turned around and looked over the neglected grounds. "This is my folks' home. They've been away for a few weeks, the gardener gone even longer as I'm sure you can tell by the state of the yard."

Samuel was Dev's stepfather? Oh, no! That meant Dev would probably be checking up on her all the time. That was the last thing she needed! Trying to keep the grimace of dismay off her face, Georgia peeked over his shoulder. The garden looked fine to her. Maybe the grass was a bit overgrown. And some of the flowers had passed their prime and obviously needed to be trimmed. But she knew nothing about gardening. Weeds, crabgrass and fertilizers were abstract concepts to her. She'd hoped to confront Samuel Williams, confirm whether he was her father, and depart before anyone discovered how inept she was.

Suddenly she realized what he'd said. If Samuel Williams was out of town, she couldn't see him today. The secretary had told her the man was away but Georgia had thought she meant away from the *office*, sick at home. How ill could he be if he had time to travel?

"I noticed," she said in the growing silence. Thoughts tumbled in her mind. When would the man return?

When Dev turned to face her, she took an involuntary step backward.

"I expect them home next weekend."

Next weekend? Today was Wednesday; that made their return nine days away. Georgia hoped her surprised dismay didn't show in her expression. She had no idea if she could pretend to be a gardener for nine whole days!

"Can you have the place in shape by then? I could have hired a landscape service, but my mother likes to have one person take care of everything. And be on hand daily to advise her when she has questions," he continued.

"Sure," she said, careful to keep all hints of her usual Southern drawl from her voice.

She dare not mention she hadn't a clue what gardening entailed. Her grandmother had had a battalion of men to care for the grounds at Beaufort Hall, where Georgia had grown up, but she had always preferred playing on the banks of the Mississippi River when a child to tagging after the yard workers.

"I assume my secretary reviewed everything with you."

Nodding, she tried to remember what they'd discussed. The impersonation had been a spur-of-the-moment attempt. She'd been so surprised the woman hired her, she hadn't paid much attention to details.

Why should she, she thought she'd be gone by night-fall.

But not if Sam Williams was away from home.

Could she stay more than a week without anyone discovering the truth? Highly unlikely.

She was so close, darn it!

Maybe Patrick or Rand would have better luck. Maybe she didn't need to talk to this man at all if either of the others proved to be her father.

Dev looked at her suspiciously. "How old are you?"

Flustered, Georgia forgot her future worry for an immediate one. How much experience would a gardener have? She'd indicated several years on her fake résumé, which meant she had to be—how old?

"How old do I look?" she asked, stalling. The dark glasses disconcerted her. She wished she could see his eyes. She could tell a lot by watching the expressions in a person's eyes.

"Twenty."

She smiled and shook her head, hoping he couldn't tell how her heart raced. "The benefit of great genes—I'm twenty-six." Well, adding four years to her real age wasn't too unbelievable, was it?

His patent look of disbelief shook her. What if he called her bluff, asked to see a driver's license or other proof of age? Or even proof she was who she said she was?

"Been gardening all your life?" he asked in mock disbelief.

Georgia nodded, trying not to fidget. Trying to remember the details of that fake résumé. If he started to cross-examine her, she'd really feel like an idiot.

But it didn't matter. If it came to that, she could always leave—and never have to see this disturbing individual again. Patrick could handle it.

But that might also mean she couldn't contact Sam Williams. This entire scheme was her idea. She had to follow it through. She dare not do less than her best after convincing Patrick and Rand to go along with the idea.

Dev slid his hands into his pockets and pulled out a small bunch of keys on a circular key ring, holding them out to her.

Georgia automatically held out her hand.

"For the shed, the mower and the garage. My secretary obviously gave you the keys for the apartment," he said.

Georgia nodded.

"Any questions?"

She shook her head, feeling as tongue-tied as a schoolgirl. Now if he would just get in that sexy car and head out, she could decide how to pretend to be a gardener for nine days.

"Come on, then. I'll show you around." Dev stood back on the small landing, waiting for her.

Georgia stepped out, too close to the man. She could feel waves of heat and energy emanating from him. Taking a breath, she drew in the tangy scent of his aftershave. And something else. Some distinctive essence that was Dev Tolliver's own. Suddenly every cell in her body seemed attuned to him.

Her reaction floored her. She almost stumbled as she hurried down the steps, astonished by the wave of pure sensual awareness that swept through her. Good grief, this man would have a hissy fit if he even suspected who she was. And she didn't want to guess what he'd do if he discovered her deception. If he threatened to call the authorities over a phone call, what would happen if he found out she had lied her way onto his stepfather's estate?

Maybe *her* father's estate as well, she reminded herself.

"This way," he said, touching her shoulder lightly.

That confusing tingling darted across her skin at his touch. Sidestepping, Georgia tried to keep a calm demeanor. She must not let him guess a mere whisper of contact affected her in any way. She felt as gauche as a first-semester nursing student flustered by some doctor. She'd survived that, so she could survive a few minutes with Dev Tolliver—as long as he didn't touch her again.

They walked around the side of the garage, along by the fence, across the grassy lawn.

"What do you think so far?" Dev asked.

Clearing her throat, she shrugged and tried to look like she was assessing the state of the grounds. Feeling she needed to say something, Georgia nodded toward a bank of roses, some already past their prime. "Nice roses."

"My mother's pride and joy. And Dad indulges her. She must have more than fifty varieties. They take a lot of care, as I'm sure you know."

"Right." Had she heard that somewhere before? Taking a breath, she decided to skip any attempt at conversation. If the only thing they had in common was flowers, she'd give herself away in an instant even if he didn't recognize her voice. She was lucky she'd identified the roses!

"This is the gardener's shed," Dev said, as they rounded a high hedge and stopped before a small wooden structure.

He waited a moment. "You have the keys."

Georgia frowned, embarrassed to be reminded. She stepped to the door and located the correct key to open the knob. Dev stood only a few feet away watching her every move. She wished she didn't feel so conscious of the man. What was wrong with her? She was used to working around dynamic men all the time. Didn't she spend her days with interns and surgeons and visiting doctors?

Opening the door, she threw it wide, gazing in bewilderment at the assortment of tools and gardening implements. The shed was immaculate.

Dev watched her, so Georgia stepped inside, a bright smile spreading. She hoped it didn't look as false as it felt. "Great, everything I need."

It was dark in the shed and when Dev stepped in, he withdrew his dark glasses. Georgia caught his gaze on her.

At least the question of his eye color was settled—silvery gray. He stared at her until she realized how many seconds were ticking by.

It was almost a physical effort to drag her gaze away to look at the huge rider-mower. Her heart raced, her palms felt damp and she had to resist the urge to look back over her shoulder at him.

She could maintain this aloof, disinterested pose until he left. Then she'd collapse on the sofa in the apartment and search for some perspective. She was not cut out for this kind of subterfuge. Undercover investigative work was not proving to be easy!

"The household staff will return on Saturday. My folks will be home the following Saturday. Does that give you enough time to get the grounds in shape?"

"Sure." Enough time to totally mess up everything if she wasn't careful. Darn it, why hadn't the secretary mentioned Samuel Williams wasn't actually in residence? Georgia would never have concocted such a wild scheme if she hadn't thought she could somehow get in to see the man today and get some answers immediately.

Dev glanced around. "I'll leave you to it until tomorrow. If you need anything, give me a call." He handed her a business card.

Georgia was a fast learner. She took the card, being careful not to let her fingers touch his. Nerves probably accounted for the wild tingling sensations, but she was not taking any more chances.

"Thanks."

She stood in the dim shed and watched him walk away. Slowly she let out her breath. Time to make some decisions. Stay or give up and return home. Maybe Patrick was right, she should have let him continue the investigation at his own pace.

Except— She wanted to know now!

Dev headed for his car, a niggling sense of something wrong tugging at his mind. Did it have to do with Georgia Brown? She struck him as nervous. And young. Definitely young. As soon as he reached the office in the morning he'd talk with Janice and review Georgia's résumé. He knew Janice would have been thorough in the interview process yet something bothered him about his mother's new gardener.

Maybe it was the fact she was so pretty. Her short blond hair looked like sunshine. Her eyes were as blue as the Gulf on a summer's day. Slim and trim, she certainly looked capable of doing the work, but there was something that just didn't mesh.

He paused by his car and glanced up at the apartment again. If his mother hadn't been so insistent about hiring a new gardener after Luis had retired, he would have contracted for a service to come in weekly. Now they had a stranger living over the garage.

Not that it mattered, but he suddenly remembered the call last week from a woman purporting to be his stepfather's long-lost daughter. They had tried to keep the extent of his dad's illness from the media. No sense making waves in the oil industry with word about how ill Samuel had been—a delayed diagnosis of acute appendicitis and the resulting toxicity because of it, which the doctors had thankfully caught in time. He was recovering and would live another forty years with luck. And be back to work within the month.

But Dev's mother was taking no chances—she'd insisted Samuel make a complete recovery before even thinking about returning! Hence their cruise.

Even so, the business sharks could smell blood. Dev had better warn Georgia to say nothing about his parents to anyone.

Heading back for the shed he rounded the corner and bumped right into her. Reaching out to steady her, he caught her arms. The soft skin beneath her short sleeves was warm and silky. Her eyes widened in surprise as she looked up into his face. For one odd moment, Dev wanted to pull her closer, wrap his arms around her and feel her warm lips beneath his.

"Oops," she said, pulling back. "I thought you'd left."

"Forgot something." Slowly he dropped his hands, closing them as if he could capture the soft texture of her skin and imprint it on his memory.

"I already locked the shed."

"It's not that. No one is to know my folks aren't home. And when they get back, no one gets in to see them unless the housekeeper admits them."

"Why?"

"I had a crackpot trying to pass herself off as Dad's daughter a few days ago. Probably heard he was ill and thought to cash in on the estate if he died. It occurs to me that she or someone like her might find out where he lives and try that way. Just be alert and don't let in strangers."

"Since everyone will be a stranger to me, I guess I wouldn't let anyone in," she said slowly. Crackpot, huh?

"There's nothing to worry about. And certainly no danger. Just be alert. Dad's still recovering and I don't want him worried with anything—especially some stranger trying a shakedown."

"Fine, no strangers trying a shakedown." She nodded.

Dev hesitated, wondering about the glint in her eyes. There was nothing more to say. Yet he was reluctant to leave. That jolt of awareness when he'd held her seemed to awaken his curiosity. He wanted to learn more about Georgia Brown. Where she was from. Why she had selected gardening as a profession.

Was there a man in her life?

"All set?" he asked, squashing the last thought. He didn't need any complications of that sort! And the last woman he'd get involved with was some charming gardener—he'd learned his lesson. If and when he was ready to start a family, he'd pick someone from his own social strata—to make sure she wasn't marrying him for his money!

She nodded again.

Fascinated despite his need to return to the office, he hesitated a moment, studying her. He noticed the faint pink color invading her cheeks—which served to make the blue of her eyes even more brilliant. He wanted to touch her again to see if her skin was as hot as it looked, or if the wash of pink was cool to the touch.

Annoyed at his sudden interest, he spun around. "I'll be here tomorrow afternoon. If you need anything before then, call the office," he said. He had to get back to work. There were still reports to read, letters to answer and that situation in the Middle East to monitor.

This time when he reached his car, he slid behind the wheel. Just before he pulled away he glanced up and saw her in the rearview mirror. She paused at the bottom of the steps to the garage apartment and stared after him.

Gunning the sports car, he took off. The next time he saw her, maybe he'd get his newest employee to say something more than a few short sentences. He found he was curious about her as he hadn't been about a woman in a long time.

Georgia waited until the sleek black car was lost from view before dashing up the stairs to her new apartment. Closing the door behind her, she leaned against it. Phew! The man was deadly. When she'd walked into him a few moments ago, she'd thought her heart would stop. His chest had been rock-hard and his reflexes lightning-swift to catch her like that.

His hands on her arms had ignited sensations she'd never experienced. For one crazy moment she'd wished he'd pulled her close and kissed her.

The imprint of his palms against her skin had awakened every feminine cell in her body. She had never felt so sexually aware of an adult male before. Or so aware of herself as a woman. She worked with men all the time, dated more than her share, had two sexy brothers-in-law. But they all paled in comparison after a few moments with Dev Tolliver.

Her heart rate gradually slowed.

At least he had not connected her with her phone call. Frowning, she pushed away from the door. His comment rankled. She was *not* some crackpot trying to cash in on her father's wealth.

She reached for the phone and quickly redialed Shelby's number.

"Hi, Patrick just called. He wants you to call him," Shelby said when she answered.

"Good, I need to talk to him. Was the New Jersey man the one we're looking for?"

"Nope."

"I guess that would have made it too easy."

It certainly would have let her off the hook.

"I know, I wish he had been the one, but Patrick was definite. Are you still at the Williams' place?"

"Yes. Give me Patrick's phone number and I'll call him."

"Then call me back and let me know what's going on."

"Will do."

"Wait a minute, Mollie wants to say hello."

Two seconds later Georgia heard Shelby's step-daughter's voice. She chatted for a few minutes with the four-year-old, remembering how quickly the little girl had taken to her at Shelby and Patrick's wedding. She already missed her. While her sister had only been married since the end of June, Georgia felt as if she'd known Mollie for ages. She planned to spend some of her vacation with her, maybe taking her to the park and the zoo.

That is, if she managed to get home before her vacation was over.

If Sam Williams didn't return until next weekend, did that mean she was stuck here until then? Was there some faster way to discover if he was her father?

As soon as she got Patrick's number, she phoned.

"So the New Jersey man isn't the right one," she said when he answered.

"No. And Rand can't get in touch with the man in California until next week."

"Well, he's not the only one. This one's away from home until next weekend. That's nine days away. There was nothing in the file about a stepson, but I met a man today who claims that distinction."

"Umm," Patrick said slowly. "Wait a minute."

Georgia heard the rustle of papers in the background.

"Here it is. Samuel Williams married a Ruth Tolliver sixteen years ago." More papers rustled. "And Ruth had a twelve-year-old son, Deveraugh Tolliver. This is her second marriage."

"Why wasn't that in the file Shelby left at my place?" Georgia wished she'd had some warning. Though would anything have prepared her for her reaction to the man?

"We were behind in the paperwork at the office because of staffing problems. I'm caught up now, but this information wasn't typed and in the file when she took it."

"I wonder if raising a son compensated for losing his daughters," she mused. "So he's still a contender."

"Not only that, he's moved up to a fifty-fifty shot. Where are you?" Patrick said.

Georgia told him, wishing she could find the humor in the situation when Patrick laughed. He didn't have to deal with Dev Tolliver.

"Now what do I do?" she asked.

"Bluff your way through. And once the house is opened, see if you can get inside and find anything that might confirm he's the one we're looking for."

"I can't break into the man's house!" Georgia was horrified.

"I'm not saying break in. Once the household staff is in place, you can deliver flowers to the various rooms. Arrange them before you take them in and get the help to let you put them where you think they'll look the best. If you start soon enough, you'll be a part of the background, so to speak, and by the end of next week they won't even notice you wandering around. Find a study or home office or check out the bedroom—the usual places people keep things.''

''Patrick, I'm not a spy, I don't know the usual places.''

''Where would *you* hide something?''

''Oh, just look there, huh?''

''It's a start. Keep in touch.''

Georgia gave him the phone number for the apartment and hung up. It looked like she was the Williams' new gardener—at least for the next week and a half. She just hoped they arrived home before she annihilated the plants and killed the grass. Somehow working in a hospital emergency room seemed far simpler in comparison.

CHAPTER TWO

BY LATE the next afternoon, Georgia was hot and cranky and bone tired. She'd figured out by trial and error how to operate the rider-mower and managed to cut the grass. Until she had gotten the knack of driving the thing, however, she'd gone off track a couple of times into the beds near the back wall—and mown down some of the flowers right down to the dirt.

She hoped she could find a nursery nearby to buy replacement plants to fill in the now gaping spots.

But not yet. She threw herself down on the apron of the pristine swimming pool she'd discovered in her exploration of the estate. Tastefully surrounded by shrubbery and a wide patio, it was a gem. Kicking off her shoes, she scooted to the edge and dangled her feet in the cool water. It felt heavenly. Sighing, she wished she'd brought a bathing suit. But except for the jeans she'd packed for casual wear, the suit she'd brought to wear when meeting Sam, and a couple of blouses, she had a very limited wardrobe.

How naive she'd been to think she could fly in one day, confront a man who, if he were her father had been successfully evading her family for more than twenty years, and be back in New Orleans within a day.

Since it looked as if she was stuck in Houston for another week, it was time to make a quick stop somewhere for clothes. And first thing she'd buy would be a bathing suit. If no one was home, how could anyone object to her using the pool?

Dumb idea, she thought. She could imagine her grandmother throwing a fit if any of the hired help had even suggested using one of the owner's amenities at Beaufort Hall. Not that they had had a pool, but the idea was the same.

"But what they don't know can't hurt them," she said, leaning back on her hands, wishing she could slip into the water and revitalize tired muscles by swimming or just plain floating on the surface.

"Making yourself at home?" a familiar, disturbing voice asked behind her.

Georgia scrambled to her feet and turned. Dev Tolliver stood only three feet away. Had he heard her talking to herself? Good grief, she'd forgotten to use her fake accent.

He'd foregone the dark glasses today, though the afternoon sun was still high enough to warrant their use. His expression was impassive, his eyes sharp. She'd give a lot to know what he was thinking.

"Sorry." New York twang firmly in place, she reached for her shoes, clutching them to her chest like a shield. "No one was home, I didn't think it'd be a problem just to see how the water felt."

She tried to sidle around him, but he put out a hand to stop her.

For a moment Georgia's mind went blank. She couldn't step away, or move closer. She could only stare at Dev, feel the warmth of his palm, and wonder if he could feel her heart race.

He looked tired. And formidable. Had he discovered her ruse? Had he seen the decimated flower beds and come to exact retribution?

"It isn't a problem," he said at last, releasing her.

"What?" Maybe she was more tired than she suspected. What was he talking about?

He shrugged and tossed a pile of mail on one of the small tables. "There won't be a problem if you use the pool when my folks aren't home. And it's hot today. Go for a swim if you like."

Georgia looked longingly at the cool water. "Thanks. But I don't have a bathing suit with me."

"Are you having your clothes sent?"

"Uh, yes. Soon."

He indicated one of the lounge chairs. "Have a seat."

Warily she sat on the edge, still holding her shoes. Lowering them to her lap she licked her dry lips. What did he want now? Any kind of conversation with the man was dangerous. She was treading a tightrope as it was and couldn't afford to give herself away.

"According to your résumé and your interview with Janice, you're from New York. But recently you were working for a family in New Orleans, the O'Shaunnessys. Why did you move here?" he asked as he placed a foot on the end of the chaise, leaning over slightly.

Georgia tried to come up with a quick answer, but he was too close. She could see the fine lines that radiated around his eyes. Feel the heat from his body, her own temperature climbing. Smell the lingering trace of his aftershave. Her insides quivered like jelly.

What was the question?

"Move here?" she asked, stalling. The secretary hadn't asked her that.

Dev said nothing, just watched her, his eyes narrowing slightly.

"My sister is about to have a baby. I want to be close to her. See the baby grow," Georgia improvised rapidly, sticking as close to the truth as she could. And it was all true, only Margot did not live in Houston.

He nodded.

She relaxed a bit. Maybe she could get through this. Unless—a horrible thought occurred to her.

"You don't live here, do you?" she asked, hoping her trepidation didn't show.

"Not normally. But I'm house-sitting while my folks are gone." He straightened and walked over to the table to pick up the stack of envelopes and catalogs. Glancing at her, he paused.

"Do you have a problem with that?"

"No, of course not."

"You get settled in okay?"

Georgia nodded. "I found a grocery store last night, so I'm all set." She still needed more clothes, but she didn't think she would share that tidbit of information. "I got started first thing this morning," she said virtuously.

"I saw the grass had been cut. It makes a big difference already."

He tapped the mail against one hand, lost in thought.

Georgia stood, ready to take flight as soon as she thought she could do so without arousing his curiosity. Warily watching him, she again noticed how tired he looked. Working too hard, she bet.

Without thinking, she said, "I'm fixing supper soon. Would you like to share it with me? If you don't have other plans. Then you could tell me more about the estate and what your mother likes in the way of flowers."

Good grief, had those words come from her mouth? *Danger, danger, danger.*

The mere thought of spending more time with him scared her. How odd would he find a newly hired employee inviting the boss to dinner?

Yet what could be a better way to casually ask questions about Samuel Williams?

"It's nothing fancy," she added as he hesitated. She'd have to be careful, but most people liked to talk about their families and if she could glean some information it would be worth the risk.

"Okay, you're on. I'll take a quick shower and change."

Walking back to her small apartment a couple of minutes later, she wondered how she could draw him out without causing any suspicions. If she succeeded, maybe she could consider a new career working as a private investigator for Patrick—if she ever got tired of nursing.

Dev showered and donned a comfortable pair of old shorts and a clean short-sleeve shirt. Work took its toll, especially doing twice the normal load in covering for his father.

Tonight offered a change of pace—eating dinner with the new gardener.

She was nothing like the women he usually dated. Not that this was a date—just a friendly invitation for a meal. It had surprised him, but maybe she was lonely.

Or was her invitation an attempt to seduce him? An attempt to attract his attention and move from gardener to something more?

He laughed and reached for the phone. Not likely. Her wide blue eyes seemed guileless and honest. She had demonstrated no evidence of flirting. It was probably only that she felt lonely and wanted some company.

And he would be glad to have a quiet meal. Lately squiring women around the expensive restaurants and nightclubs downtown had paled. He still had the occasional function to attend that would help generate more business, or keep current customers happy. But they no longer held the same appeal or excitement as they once had.

He dialed the garage apartment.

"Hello?"

"Georgia?" Did the sound of her voice jog a memory?

"Yes."

He was imagining things. That New York accent was particularly her own.

"Dev here. I thought we could eat by the pool, if you like."

"Why sure, if that's allowed. I made a chef's salad and heated some rolls. I think there'll be enough to fill you up. I'll bring it over."

"I'll be there in a minute to help you carry the things out."

"Okay."

Satisfied there would be no romantic overtones to the meal, Dev headed for the garage.

Entering her apartment a few minutes later, he looked around. He could not see any appreciable difference to the room except for the small bouquet of roses on the coffee table—the blossoms past their prime. Odd, she hadn't done more to make the place her own. Of course she'd only been here a day. Probably her personal things were coming with her clothes.

"Nice flowers," he commented.

She flushed and nodded. "They're a bit past their peak, but I didn't want to just let them wither on the branch. And they still smell fragrant."

Just like a gardener, he thought, couldn't let go of flowers.

"Take some fresh ones next time," he said. "My mother loves to have fresh flowers in the house."

He thought she looked startled for a moment, but put it down to imagination when she looked away and said, "Great, I'll be sure and have some at the house when she returns. I'll do arrangements for every room. Maybe the housekeeper can give me a tour when she gets back."

"Or I can later."

She nodded, and then gestured to a small tray laden with plates and glasses.

"The salad is ready and the rolls will be done in another minute or two. Want to carry out the plates and iced tea?"

Settled on the apron of the pool a few minutes later,

shaded from the sinking sun by one of the huge umbrellas his mother insisted on, Dev began to relax. It was quiet and peaceful. Georgia sat across the small table. She had not made eye contact once. Toying with her food, she seemed ill at ease. She wore her jeans, but had obviously taken time to shower. Her hair was still a bit damp, and her shirt fresh and clean.

And hugging her figure. Her very feminine, delectable figure. Outdoor work must be good for keeping muscles toned, and weight off. She looked fit and sexy.

"Aren't you hungry?" he asked as she took another sip of tea. He needed something to take his mind off that line of thought. He had no business thinking about her figure!

"Actually, I nibbled a bit while preparing the salad," she confessed. "I was starved then. Is this enough for you? I expect being from Texas, you'd much rather eat beef."

"And being from New York, you'd probably prefer a Coney Island hot dog."

She smiled and shook her head. "I like salads. Will it fill you up?"

"With the rolls." He looked at her. "Thanks for dinner."

"So tell me all about yourself," she invited a minute or two later as the silence stretched out.

Suddenly going on the alert, Dev put his fork down. "What exactly do you want to know?"

"What it was like growing up here? Did you play football? Did your stepfather coach Little League? Did he teach you to swim? Whatever."

Dev relaxed again. "I didn't grow up here. My

folks only bought this place during my last year of high school. Before that we lived closer to Galveston. Yes, I played some ball in high school, but didn't in college. I like to swim, but I learned to do that before my mother married Samuel. The pool is Dad's pride and joy, however."

Dev launched into a tale about how his dad convinced his mother to agree to a pool. And then how he and Samuel had *helped* the contractor—causing more problems than they solved. He had a way of making Georgia feel she was right there. And he made his stepfather sound like a perfect parent, caring, and yet able to let Dev make some of his own mistakes.

Laughing at one of his comments, she felt a pang that she'd missed out on that kind of relationship with her father.

"Tell me more about yourself. Were you born and raised in New York?" he asked a few minutes later.

She hesitated. For a moment, she almost told him the truth, wanted to tell him the truth—but she had experienced his reaction to her phone call, she couldn't risk discovery at this point. Slowly she nodded.

"I always think of New York as glass and concrete."

"There are nice areas with gardens and yards," she said.

"Are you and your sister the only ones?"

"I have two sisters," Georgia said slowly, feeling she was walking a tightrope between the truth and pretense.

Dev took his roll and broke off a piece, buttering it. "What do your parents do?"

"I never knew them. My mother died right after I was born and...my father had gone before her."

"That's tough. I'm sorry."

She nodded.

"My mother divorced my real father when I was just a little kid. She married Samuel when I was twelve. I think of him as my father. He and I are closer than my mother and I." Dev popped the roll into his mouth, wondering why he'd told Georgia that bit of information. It was not something he normally talked about to strangers—or even friends for that matter.

"Then lucky you. Our grandmother raised us."

"I have been lucky. You'll like him when you meet him. He's fair and honest. Works hard. Plays hard, too. And he's crazy about my mother. Which helps make up for her first marriage. It wasn't that happy."

"Is this your Dad's first marriage?" she asked casually, tracing a pattern on the condensation of her glass.

Dev looked at her sharply. "Yes," he said.

"Tell me about your family vacations. Where was the best spot your parents took you?" she said, quickly changing the subject.

For the next few minutes, Dev regaled her with outlandish stories of his childhood, embellished from time to time to impress such an avid listener. He spoke often of his parents, sharing his memories with a woman who didn't have the same kind of memories.

Growing silent, he looked over at her. The sun was

sinking behind the trees. Twilight would descend soon. The evening had sped by.

She looked up then and met his gaze. Her eyes were serious. Leaning forward slightly, she smiled. "If you go inside now, I could come back here later and go skinny-dipping. That pool still looks mighty inviting."

Dev smiled. Gotcha, he thought. She was just like the others, a little slower in making her move, that was all.

"What if I stay?" he suggested provocatively.

Her smile faded. Her manner became distant. "Then I'll have to wait until I get a bathing suit, I guess. I'll take a warm bath to relax instead. Are you finished?"

"Yes."

"Then, good night." She stood and began stacking the dishes.

"I'll help take the things in with you."

She looked at him, consideringly. Shaking her head slowly, she picked up the tray with their stacked dishes. "I can manage. Thanks for sharing dinner with me. I get lonely sometimes at mealtimes. The rest of the time, I'm fine. But eating alone isn't all that much fun."

He watched her walk toward the garage apartment, her head held high, balancing the heavy tray as if were light as a feather.

So much for thinking Georgia Brown was like anyone else he'd ever met. He'd thought her comment about skinny-dipping was her way of suggesting their relationship take another direction. He'd misread the signs.

She intrigued him, no denying that. Stretching out on the lounge chair, he leaned back. He was tired. Fielding his own calls and his father's, keeping the company on an even keel, trying to juggle the myriad of unfamiliar tasks while doing his own workload was challenging—exciting, but also draining. Tonight was a rare evening since his father left the hospital that he hadn't stayed at the office until long after dark.

Though maybe dinner could have been considered working late—interviewing a new employee. Except now that he thought about their conversation, he'd done more of the talking. He still didn't feel he knew Georgia Brown. What made her tick? Why had she left the place where she'd been born and raised to move first to New Orleans, then follow a sister to Houston? He hadn't learned anything about her sister.

But he had learned Georgia could listen like she hung on every word he uttered. That her wide blue eyes could look at a man like he was special, without flirting or teasing.

And her laugh enchanted him.

Frowning, Dev studied the pool. He was *not* enchanted. He was mildly interested in the new gardener—nothing more!

Maybe tomorrow he'd leave work early enough to invite her out to dinner in return for tonight's meal. And see what else he could discover.

Georgia quickly cleaned up after the meal. Turning off the light in the tiny kitchen, she gazed out over the yard. Lights now illuminated the pool area and some of the flower beds visible from her window. But she couldn't see Dev. Was he still sitting by the water, or had he gone inside?

Tempted to sneak near the pool to check it out, she firmly squelched the idea. She wanted to swim, but not enough to risk running into him again tonight. If she only knew if his stepfather was her real father, things would be different. She'd have some idea about how to handle things.

But right now, everything was too uncertain. And she couldn't afford to be discovered. Not until she had a chance to meet Sam.

Dev's tales of his childhood haunted her. He spoke with such love and affection about both his mother and Samuel. Her only childhood memories were of her grandmother's rather stern ideas of raising girls to be ladies. There had been no family camping vacations, no trips to the beach or Disney World.

Not that it mattered now. She had a good job, could afford to go wherever she wanted for vacation.

"Yeah, right. So how come you're in Houston?" she asked as she wandered into the bedroom. Taking off her jeans, she lay down on the bed, trying to relax her muscles. She was used to hard work—lifting patients, carrying heavy trays of medicines, making beds, on her feet all day. But today she'd used some different muscles and now paid the price.

Maybe later she'd see if the pool was deserted, but right now she was too tired to even move.

It was after midnight when Georgia awoke. She moved restlessly on the bed, her back and shoulders aching.

Sitting up, she pulled on her jeans and caught a towel from the bathroom. Walking across the dark yard to the pool she checked out the house to make sure no lights were on. Dev was sound asleep, she knew. The outdoor lights had to be on a timer. They were no longer illuminating the pool or gardens.

Slipping off her jeans and shirt at the edge of the pool, she slipped into the inviting water, wearing only a bra and panties.

The coolness felt great against her heated skin. Slowly, making as little noise as possible, she swam for a while, then flipped over and floated. The stars were brilliant against the dark velvet of the night sky, the moon was just a sliver in the western horizon. August nights in Houston were just as hot and humid as in New Orleans. Georgia enjoyed the refreshing cool water against her skin.

It was late by the time she reluctantly climbed from the pool. Dripping, she wrung water from her hair. It wouldn't take long for the sultry heat to evaporate the water from her skin and hair. Feeling refreshed, relaxed and ready for sleep, she picked up her jeans and shirt and wandered back to her apartment enjoying the quiet night.

Would she be able to take advantage of the pool when the rest of the household returned?

If not officially, she could always sneak in after everyone was asleep.

Bright and early the next morning Georgia planned her day. First thing she needed to do was to find a clothing store, then a nursery. She counted on the nursery carrying books on gardening that she could read up enough to pass muster to any casual questions. Though her goal was to stay away from people who would ask them.

She didn't trust the gleam she'd seen in Dev's eye. He was too astute. If she slipped, he'd pounce on any mistake instantly.

And send her packing.

Which she didn't want.

Because of the need to see Sam Williams, she told herself firmly. It had nothing to do with wishing to see Dev again. Though if he came home early tonight, maybe she'd just happen to be in the yard. And if she thought of ordering pizza on the spur of the moment, could he fault her for that?

Opening the door a few minutes later, she stopped at the sight of the neatly folded towel she'd forgotten by the pool. A note rested on top.

His handwriting was bold. *It's dangerous to swim alone. Next time wake me*!

Slipping the note into her pocket, Georgia almost laughed. As if it wouldn't be twice as dangerous to go swimming after midnight with a man like Dev Tolliver!

Georgia thought about him as she went through the day. What would have happened if they met under different circumstances? Would he even look at a nurse? From the few things he'd mentioned last evening, she knew he was used to dating more sophisticated women—the kind her grandmother had tried so hard to mold Georgia into.

Not that it mattered. Once she left Houston, she'd never see Dev again.

It was odd how the thought caused feelings of disappointment and regret.

By seven that evening, Georgia gave up. He was not coming by the house as she had hoped. There was only so much she could pretend to be doing and not get dirty. She'd cleaned up at four, donned one of the new shorts and sleeveless tops she'd bought that morning. Just a hint of makeup to enhance her eyes and she'd been set.

Carefully cutting dead blossoms, she began working near the garage. It was Friday night. He probably had a date. But just in case, she wanted to be in the vicinity if he arrived home.

Gradually moving along the fence, she now worked behind the house and still no sign of Dev's fancy sports car. She might as well call for that pizza and find another way to spend her evening. He wasn't showing up after all.

"Which is just as well," she mumbled as she put away the clippers and dumped the dead flowers in the compost pile she'd found behind the shed. "You have no business getting involved at all with Samuel Williams' stepson. Identify the man, and take it from there. If he's your father, what next?"

She stopped dead, suddenly realizing she hadn't a clue what she and her sisters would do once they located the man. Vaguely there had been talk about making sure he wasn't in want.

If this man was their father, he was definitely not in want.

No one had even considered he might not wish to see them. But now Georgia wondered. Would he, like Dev, think they were after his money?

She shivered despite the warm evening. How awful for people to suspect others couldn't like you for yourself, but only because of your money.

Or family position—her grandmother's view of life.

Maybe Georgia would verify the relationship and slip away without saying anything. She could report back to Margot and Shelby and the three of them could decide what to do next.

Georgia ordered pizza, picked up the gardening book she'd purchased that morning and sat in the only easy chair in the apartment. *Step-by-Step to a Perfect Garden* seemed as basic as she could get. Beginning at Chapter One she was halfway through it when the knock came on the door.

The pizza. She was hungry. Putting down the book, she grabbed her purse and hurried to the door. Opening it, she was astonished to see Dev standing there—holding a pizza box.

"Pizza delivery," he said easily. Without waiting for an invitation, he stepped inside.

Georgia looked in the driveway. Only Dev's car was visible.

"How did you get the pizza?" she asked, slowly closing the door behind her. He'd already gone into the kitchen.

"Met the guy just as I was pulling in. Thought maybe you'd take pity on a hardworking man and offer to share." He stood in the doorway. "Especially since I paid for it."

"I'll pay you back," she said, reaching for her wallet.

"You don't want to share?"

Georgia had spent all day planning how she'd casually ask him to join her for dinner. She almost laughed aloud at his question. Feigning indifference, she shrugged. "It's fine with me. But you didn't get a chance to choose toppings."

"I peeked. Looks great. I'm not sure it'll be enough for both of us, but we can order a second one if we want."

"I didn't expect company," she said, laying down her purse and heading for the kitchen. "If I had known you would be home, I would have ordered a larger one."

She grabbed plates, napkins and glasses. Dev pulled a pitcher of iced tea from the refrigerator. Just as if he'd been doing it forever, she thought as she set the small table in the breakfast nook.

"Did you just finish work?" she asked when they were seated. He had discarded his suit jacket somewhere, loosened his tie and rolled back the sleeves of his shirt, revealing muscular arms. His dark hair was mussed, as if he'd run his fingers through it in frustration.

Georgia didn't like the way her body began to react around him. She was here on a mission, not to fall for some sexy Texan.

"I feel I'm doing two jobs with Dad out. I had some department managers in this afternoon for a planning session. It ran late." He looked at her, his eyes silvery in the light. "Actually, this is the second day I've left early since Dad's been out."

Blood thundered in her veins. Dev didn't say it, but she knew he meant he'd left early because of her.

"Oh."

Slowly he smiled and Georgia felt her insides begin to melt.

CHAPTER THREE

FLUSTERED, Georgia didn't like the feeling. She needed to be in complete control so she would give nothing away!

"So, your father will be home soon, and then you'll just have your job to do, right?"

"He'll be home soon, but I'm not sure when he'll be back to a full load at the office."

"He was ill, I think you said." Had Dev mentioned it? Or had it been the secretary who had told her that? "Nothing life-threatening, I hope."

"Appendicitis with complications. He'll be fine."

The pizza was good and Georgia had no trouble eating her share. If Dev didn't want to talk, she was certainly not going to fill the silence. Too aware of where her tongue could lead her, she knew discretion was the better path for her.

"If you didn't want me to crash dinner, you could have said so," he said a few moments later.

She met his gaze, trying to ignore the rampant sensations that filled her with just a look from the man. What would happen if he touched her again? Caught her close and kissed her?

Heat washed through her, and she knew her skin flushed. She'd give anything to be impervious to such reactions. Her fair skin was the bane of her existence. She had to remember he was her new employer— nothing more! No kisses!

"I'm glad to have you stay," she said primly. If he only knew!

"But?"

She shook her head and smiled. "But nothing. I'm just not sure what to say." What to say that wouldn't give her away.

"Then tell me about swimming in the middle of the night," he suggested, amusement dancing in his eyes.

"I didn't expect to be caught out," she said, laughing softly. "I just couldn't resist. And if I hadn't forgotten the towel, you would have never known."

"Makes me wonder what else goes on around here that I don't know about," he said easily.

Guilt had her dropping her gaze to her pizza. They were down to the last piece. Would Dev leave as soon as he ate, or stay a bit longer? What did she want him to do?

"Do you want a blow-by-blow account of my day?" Georgia asked playfully.

"I don't think I need it. I can see a difference in the yard's appearance already. Keep it up and the place will be perfect when Mom and Dad return."

An unexpected feeling of satisfaction spread through her at his words. She'd done very little, actually, more afraid of messing up than helping. But some of the shaggy appearance of the flowers had disappeared when she cut the dead blossoms. And with the grass taken care of, the entire estate looked better—even she acknowledged it. Thank goodness the rider-mower was so easy to use—once she'd figured out how to steer it!

"Did you have enough, or should I order more?" Dev asked when he finished the last piece of pizza.

"I'm full. You're the one who could probably use more," Georgia replied.

"It'll hold me for a while."

"Thanks for buying it," she said shyly.

He shrugged. "Actually, I called you a couple of times today. I was going to ask you out to dinner— my turn after last night."

"Oh. I guess I was outside working." She just hoped he didn't expect to see miraculous improvement in the yard after all her supposed hours working!

"Maybe you should carry a cell phone so people can reach you during the day."

"I hardly think that is necessary," Georgia said with a smile. Sounded like a high-powered businessman—never be out of touch.

"What if your sister calls to say the baby's coming?"

"Margot? She couldn't—" Almost too late Georgia realized the pitfall. Margot didn't know where she was, or what she was doing. She thought Georgia was taking a few days of vacation to visit with friends.

"Couldn't?"

"*Wouldn't* call me during work time. Besides, the baby isn't due until the second week in November."

"Her first?"

"She was pregnant before, and miscarried. We're trying to make sure she delivers a healthy baby this time."

"Are you a doctor?" Dev joked. "How are you making sure she delivers a healthy baby?"

"Mostly by making sure she hasn't a thing to worry about," Georgia said, standing. She needed to change the subject.

"I found some strawberries in that plot behind the shrubbery on the far side of the pool. Want some with ice cream?" she asked, reaching for his plate.

His hand circled her wrist, holding her in place. "Swiping produce now?"

Her heart tripping double time, Georgia could scarcely breathe. His touch wreaked havoc with her senses. His hand was warm and firm, his fingers stroking her lightly, but the shivering sensations that danced on her skin disturbed her equilibrium. Gazing into his silvery eyes, Georgia longed to drop the plate and move closer. Forgotten was the need for secrecy, for subterfuge. For one crazy moment she wanted to explore the excitement of being with Dev Tolliver.

When his thumb brushed lightly against the soft inner skin of her arm, Georgia knew she was going to blow everything if she didn't put some distance between them.

Tugging her wrist free, she stepped back.

"I didn't want them to go to waste," she said breathlessly. Get a grip, she told herself as she stepped into the minuscule kitchen.

"Can I help?" Dev was right behind her. She imagined she could feel the warmth from his body encase her. The kitchen wasn't big enough for two people to move around without bumping into each other.

"No, I'm fine. I can manage."

He reached around her and opened the cupboard door, taking down two bowls. Once again Georgia was struck with how he fit in the apartment. How they worked together as if choreographed.

She withdrew the ice cream from the freezer and Dev took it from her hands. In only a moment, he had scooped it into the two bowls. She produced the sliced strawberries.

"Want to take them out to the pool?" he asked.

"No. Let's just sit inside." And when he was done, maybe he'd leave and let her get herself under control!

"Want coffee?"

"I'd take some more iced tea," he said heading for the living room.

Grateful for something to do, Georgia fixed them both fresh glasses.

"What's this?" Dev asked when she entered the room a few minutes later. In his hand was the gardening book she'd been reading.

Stunned, Georgia stared at it. Endless seconds later she looked at Dev. His expression gave nothing away. He must be great in business, she thought wildly, nothing escaped his notice.

Frantically, she tried to think. Placing his glass near him, she took hers to the chair opposite. He'd set her ice cream bowl near him, but she couldn't sit that close. Reaching for it she tried smiling. Would her cheeks crack?

"I, um, was a, ah, contributor to the book. I got a copy to see how things turned out."

"I'm impressed. Which part was yours?"

"Which part?" Georgia scrambled for an idea. Staring at the book, her mind went blank.

"Did you do a chapter or something?" Dev asked, watching her oddly.

"Oh, no. I worked with one of the writers on several sections. That's all."

He glanced at the spine. "You aren't listed."

"No. Umm, I sort of researched things for one of the authors. Suggested the outline of the section on, uh, annuals." She trailed off, not having any idea what she was talking about. Was there a section on annuals in that particular book? She hoped so.

"Do you do this kind of thing often?"

"No. I prefer to work outside. Anyway, it's done now, and I doubt I'll collaborate on any other books."

"How did it turn out?"

"What?"

"Your input to the book."

"I just started reading it today. So far so good." Smiling inanely, Georgia longed to change the subject. What would be compelling enough to get him off the subject of the blasted book! If she'd suspected he was planning to drop by, she'd have hidden it beneath the pillow in her bedroom. The last thing she needed was for Dev to see her reading a gardener's book for beginners.

Dev put the book down and picked up his ice cream again. "So, planning any more midnight swims?"

Georgia wanted to close her eyes and sink through the floor. Maybe his visit could end soon. The book was bad enough, now he was reminding her of that. She couldn't forget his offer to join her if she went again.

"No." She took a spoonful of ice cream.

"Let me know when you get your bathing suit, we can use the pool one evening."

"Ump."

When pigs fly. There was no way she was going to tell him she'd bought a swimsuit today. She was already too susceptible around the man. The last thing she needed was to see him in swim trunks. Or did he wear those Speedos?

Georgia had a working knowledge of the human body from all her anatomy classes. Which only aided her in imagining Dev in a swimsuit. With his broad shoulders and muscular built, she bet he was a knock-out. He was gorgeous enough in business attire. She didn't think she should get within fifty feet of him without his clothes.

But the image danced before her eyes, tempting her to agree.

She cleared her throat. "So the rest of the staff returns tomorrow?" she asked.

"Yes. Mrs. Mitton is the housekeeper. She lives in. Thelma Fields is the cook. You'll love her food. She cooks for the entire household, so if you want, you can have your meals there. Mrs. Mitton has a couple of women in during the week to help with the laundry and housework."

"I look forward to meeting them," she said politely.

The amusement danced in his eyes again.

"Did I say something funny?" she asked, puzzled.

"Sometimes you sound like some prissy debutante. Other times you're open and forthright. And yet, I detect a hint of something mysterious about you, Georgia Brown. Who are you really?"

"My grandmother drilled good manners into us. Is that a crime?" She didn't want to touch the subject of who she was. He'd have a fit if he found out. She couldn't let that happen.

"No crime. It all adds up to an intriguing woman."

Oh gosh, the last thing she needed was him to become interested in learning more about her. She needed space and freedom.

"If you're finished, I'll take your bowl," she said, jumping to her feet, torn between wanting to spend time with Dev because he was the most desirable man she'd ever met, and the need to get him out before the conversation took another personal turn.

"In a hurry for me to leave?" he asked, rising.

"Not at all. But I'm sure you have things to do. I'm surprised you don't have a date tonight. I can't expect to monopolize your time. Thanks for stopping by and for the pizza and everything."

Dev ran his hand around the back of his neck, then stretched. Georgia watched, fascinated, wishing suddenly she had taken him up on the swimming offer.

"No date tonight," he said shortly. "I enjoyed the pizza and the ice cream."

"Thank you. You bought it."

"So I did." He took a step closer. "So if I bought dinner, maybe *this* was my date for tonight."

She couldn't move. Clenching the bowls tightly in her hands, she wanted to dash away, and at the same time, step closer.

"Short date."

"Fun, too." Slowly he leaned closer until his face filled her vision.

He was going to kiss her, and Georgia didn't know

what to do. Frantically she tried to decide what would be the better plan, give in, or run away. Taking too long, she ended up doing nothing except slowly letting her eyes close.

The touch of his lips was wonderful. Warm and firm, they moved against hers in a kiss that zapped her knees and made it difficult for her to stand. *Don't drop the bowls*, was the only thought that filtered through the raging delight that consumed her.

All too soon, he stepped back.

"If you change your mind about swimming later, let me know. My room is the corner one in the back."

With that he left.

Georgia stared after him in a bemused trance for several minutes. Her lips still felt the pressure of his. Her heart raced and danced. Her hands grew numb clenching the ice cream bowls. Blinking, she gradually became aware of standing in the empty living room.

Had he really kissed her?

Smiling, she almost waltzed into the kitchen. He had, and she liked it!

Dev grabbed his briefcase and suit jacket from the car. He glanced at the garage apartment once more before heading for the main house, his senses on alert. Something was odd about Georgia Brown. Odd and fascinating. She was a contradiction that he didn't understand—yet.

He strode across the yard, noticing the changes she'd wrought. At least she was making a start. He hoped the grounds were back in order by the time his mother saw them.

As he skirted the pool, he remembered finding the towel that morning, and knowing Georgia had gone swimming alone. For a moment, the image of her sleek body moving through the water had strengthened his resolve to get to know her better.

He was wary around women who tried to play games. More often than not, a woman wanted to be seen with him, to enhance her own status in the world. He was generous, liked to have a good time and didn't mind being used as a status symbol. But he wasn't planning to settle down with anyone who could be a fortune hunter. After all, his near brush with matrimony with his former fiancée had taught him that lesson.

Not that he was thinking about marriage—just a few evenings in the company of Georgia Brown. She intrigued him—shy one moment, funny the next, with interesting odd slants on things. There was more to her than he at first suspected.

Dev unlocked the door to the kitchen and entered. Walking through to the study, he placed the day's mail in the growing pile, and set his briefcase on the floor beside the desk. Tomorrow, he'd work from the study to make sure he was home when Mrs. Mitton returned. And Thelma. Both women had been given paid vacations while his stepfather and mother took that cruise.

Dev hoped the extended trip had worked as his mother wanted and that Samuel was returning in much improved health. Dev had done his best to shelter him from everything—to enable him to devote his full energy toward recovery.

Taking the stairs two at a time, Dev headed for his

room. Too early to go to bed, but not too early to change and head for the pool. Would she come tonight despite her statement to the contrary? Or would he wait in vain?

Dev awoke, immediately alert. He lay on one of the lounge chairs beyond the circle of light from the pool. The light that was no longer on, he noticed. Glancing at his watch, he saw it was after one. The night was dark, clouds drifted across the stars, throwing moving shadows across the lawn, the surface of the water.

He rubbed his face. She wasn't coming after all. Just as she had said. He might as well take a final swim and head for bed. He'd been so sure she'd show up.

Just then he heard the swish of someone walking on the grass.

Georgia stepped onto the cool concrete surrounding the pool and hesitated. Dev could see her outlined against the night stars. She seemed to peer toward the house. He had not left a light burning.

She dropped a towel on a chair and pulled her T-shirt over her head. For a moment he held his breath. She wore a sleek one-piece bathing suit. It clung to her skin lovingly, outlining the curves and valleys faithfully.

Then a cloud blotted the faint light and she was lost to sight, just a vague silhouette against the sky.

When she plunged into the water, Dev's anger flashed. She should know better than to go swimming alone. Why hadn't she called him?

Because she wasn't playing games to entice him.

She said what she felt, and she had not wanted him here.

Tough. He rose and touched the switch that turned on the underwater pool lights.

Georgia shot straight to the surface.

"Oh my gosh, you scared me half to death!" Her voice was almost a yell when she saw him at the edge. Treading water, she slicked back her hair and glared at him.

"You can see better with the lights on," he said mildly.

"I was doing fine."

Dev made a shallow dive, surfacing right in front of her.

"I see you found a suit. Or did your clothes arrive?"

"I bought it today. You said I could use the pool." Treading water, she moved back a few feet. Dev followed.

"I'm not complaining about that, but about your swimming alone."

"Okay. I'm not alone now," she said, kicking back and starting to swim again. Dev paced her as they moved up and down the long pool. She was serious about swimming and he enjoyed the workout. Hadn't she said she wanted to relax her muscles? It worked with his own as well.

Stopping at last, Georgia made to climb out of the shallow end.

"Don't go yet," Dev said, standing beside her. For a moment he felt her gaze on his chest. Enjoyed the way her eyes widened as she studied him. When she looked away, he wanted her to look back. Crazy.

"Georgia?"

"I've got to go now. Thanks for the swim."

Not even thinking, just reacting, Dev reached for her before she could leave. He pulled her cool body into his arms, holding her tight enough to mold her soft form against his harder one. Her lips were cool, initially. But after his moved against hers, they warmed.

Softly he traced her curves, feeling the edge of her suit, the silky texture of her back. The wet strands of her hair tangled with his fingers. Deepening the kiss, Dev was unaware of time drifting by. He wanted this woman. Her body seemed a perfect match to his and her kisses inflamed him. The touch of her hands against his shoulders, his chest ignited a conflagration that the pool water couldn't extinguish.

When she pushed against him, he reluctantly released her.

"I don't think that was such a great idea," she said, sloshing through the water to the shallow steps in the corner.

"Why not?"

"You're too dangerous," she muttered, rising from the pool, water streaming from her.

Dev stood still, glad the water covered his body's reaction to her. She found him *dangerous*? Then he smiled. Suddenly he knew she didn't mean in a threatening manner. At least not threatening in a physical sense.

"Care to clarify that?"

She stopped drying her hair with the towel and looked at him.

"As if you needed any clarification. You probably have women dropping like flies at your feet."

Dev roared with laughter. "Such an appealing picture. Flies?"

"You know what I mean," she snapped. Wrapping the towel around her waist, she yanked on her T-shirt.

He vaulted from the side of the pool, and walked over to her before she could leave. Away from the pool, the light was fainter. But he could see her clearly enough to recognize the wariness with which she regarded him.

"It was just a kiss, Georgia."

"Yes, I know. And I want to keep it at just a kiss. Good night, Dev." She turned and hurried into the dark yard.

"Here's the game plan," Georgia muttered to herself as she almost ran to her apartment. "Do all you can to find out about Samuel Williams, and stay as far away from Dev as you can!"

She glanced over her shoulder. "And no more kisses," she whispered, wondering if she would be able to resist if he offered more.

First thing Saturday morning, Georgia skimmed as much of the gardening book as she could. Before going swimming the previous night, she'd read several chapters. She now had a nodding acquaintance with gardening and if she could just hold on and appear to be doing something until the Williamses returned home, she'd be set.

Dressed in loose shorts and a light cotton top, she headed outside. She'd seen a station wagon arrive some time ago. One of the household staff members, she bet. When the old car had shown up, she knew she should go and introduce herself. Maybe once everyone was in place, Dev would remember she worked for his father and establish some boundaries. After all she was the hired help. Shouldn't he keep his distance?

No such luck today. He was lounging in the kitchen chatting with the two older women when Georgia knocked on the door. Within ten minutes, all four sat around the kitchen table like old friends. Thelma had brought fresh-baked cookies with her.

"Knowing I wouldn't have time to bake any before someone demanded something sweet to eat," she said, smiling at Dev.

"I miss your cooking," he said with a shrug, reaching for another cookie.

Georgia watched, fascinated. For a moment she could imagine him as a teenager, mischievous and charming, able to wrap the cook around his little finger.

"As if you come to visit often enough to enjoy it."

"I may be here more than you think the next few weeks," he said, glancing at Georgia.

She tried to ignore him, ignore her clamoring senses. Hadn't she vowed to keep her distance just a few hours ago?

"How do you like working here?" Mrs. Mitton asked Georgia.

"Fine. The yard is lovely, or will be soon. And the apartment is great."

"Now don't go fixing your own meals when you can eat with us," Thelma said.

Georgia smiled, knowing she wouldn't be here long enough to establish any routine.

"Georgia's promised to make sure there are plenty of flowers in the house when Mother gets home," Dev said, as if challenging her to ignore him any longer.

She nodded. "If you tell me which rooms you'd like arrangements in, I'll see to it," she said, addressing Mrs. Mitton.

Before that woman could respond, Dev stood.

"Come with me, Georgia. I'll give you a grand tour. Then you can see which color combinations and flowers would work in each room."

He held out his hand, but she ignored it—wishing she could ignore the hint of command behind his suggestion.

Mrs. Mitton looked surprised, then she exchanged glances with Thelma. Both smiled.

Georgia wanted to make it perfectly clear that nothing was going on, but she dare not argue against something that had never been voiced.

"Mrs. Mitton could have shown me," she said a minute later when Dev led the way down the wide hallway to the open foyer.

"Ah, but this is my home, I can show you so much better, don't you think?"

"I thought this was your stepfather's home."

He hesitated a moment, and studied her with wary eyes. "It belongs to him, but it's my home, too."

Georgia looked around. The foyer was large, with a curving stairway that led to the second story. Through a wide archway, she could see the elegant living room. Cream and gold and blue were the dominant colors. She stepped to the arch and admired the decor. While it was sumptuous, it was also inviting. Welcoming. So unlike the formal parlor in her grandmother's house.

Dev led her into the room, pointing out locations he knew his mother liked filled with flowers. Next came the dining room.

"And that room?" Georgia asked in passing at the door, partially ajar.

"That's Dad's study."

"Does he like flowers? I could do an arrangement for that room as well," she said, wishing she could glimpse inside. Would there be old records, letters, something to tie Dev's father to the Sam Williams who had once married Amanda Beaufort and been forced to abandon his family twenty-three years ago?

CHAPTER FOUR

"No NEED for flowers in there—it's a working office." Dev touched her shoulder lightly, urging her into the dining room.

It was a spacious, elegant room with a stately table which would seat twelve centered beneath a huge crystal chandelier. The rich cherry wood gleamed. Had Mrs. Mitton begun working already, or was the house kept in excellent condition despite the housekeeper's absence?

"How long ago did your father become ill?" she asked, touching the satiny finish.

"Several weeks, why?"

"The house is immaculate. I wondered how long Mrs. Mitton had been gone."

"The staff was given a three-week vacation when my parents left for their cruise. Don't you think I've been dusting and keeping things up?" he asked. A gleam in his eyes told her he was teasing.

Georgia laughed and shook her head. "Nope. Never for one minute."

He frowned. "How can you say that? I could have worked my fingers to the bone every night after work."

"I can see you ordering minions about, but not participating in such mundane tasks."

"I keep my own place tidy—but I do have a cleaning service which comes in once a week."

66

"See, a single person doesn't mess up their own place enough to need a service."

"Maybe *need* is strong, maybe it's just that I like having it."

And can indulge yourself, she thought, looking away before she said something inappropriate. Why not? Truth to tell if she made enough money, she'd probably indulge herself by having someone come in once a week, too. Not that it took that much effort to dust and vacuum her small apartment, but still, the luxury of having someone else do it was appealing.

"My mother likes big bouquets on the sideboard. Roses are her favorites."

"So you said," Georgia murmured, studying the antique furniture. She would love to see quantities of fragrant blossoms add their color to the room. She'd also love to see the room filled with guests, laughing, enjoying Thelma's cooking, and sharing amusing anecdotes of their lives.

"So what else?" she asked briskly, damping down her imagination. She wouldn't be here long enough to even glimpse a party through the window, much less attend one. Once she had her answer, she'd be gone.

Glancing at Dev, she frowned. For some reason the thought of leaving was disquieting.

"The small sunroom." Dev led the way. "My mother spends a lot of time here. Of course with all the glass, she can see much of the garden already." He paused in the doorway. Georgia peeked around him. White wicker furnishings were scattered in a casual array. The solid glass walls seemed to bring the outdoors in, making it a part of the room.

She saw the spot where she'd mowed down the flowers and winced. She had to get something to replace the ones she'd ruined before his mother arrived. It might be better to wait for Friday so if in transplanting the flowers from the pots to the ground she did something wrong and they died, she would be gone before it became noticeable.

"There's a sitting room upstairs off the master bedroom which my mother uses a lot—to read or write letters. A small vase up there would be nice."

Georgia went on alert. A room right off the master bedroom? How perfect. She now had a reason to be in all parts of the house for the search Patrick suggested.

"Can I see that, too?" she asked, hoping her excitement didn't show.

"Sure." Dev led the way up the curving stairs. He turned left at the top and opened a door into a beautiful, feminine room. The priscilla curtains on the windows were sparkling white and crisp. The damask rose-colored chaise-longue invited someone to recline, read, or just dream. The Queen Anne furniture added to the romantic setting—lovely and delicate.

Georgia gazed around the room. A strong yearning filled her. She'd love to have a room like this where she could retreat, make plans or just daydream.

Through an open door, she glimpsed a bed—the master bedroom.

"Where's your bedroom?" she asked, turning to face him. "Now that we're on this level, I might as well see everything, right?" She couldn't explain her curiosity. Dev would provide nothing she needed to further her quest, but that didn't stop her from being interested in everything about the man.

"Across the hall. But I warn you, no flowers. The room still looks like it did when I left for college." He pushed open a door to a room across the hall from his parents.

Georgia smiled when she stepped in. It looked like a teenager's room. Posters of racing cars and pop musicians hung on the wall. Notebooks were stacked haphazardly on crowded shelves. She walked over to study the trophies on one shelf—all for swimming events.

"I ought to clear it out and start over," he said from the doorway.

Georgia looked over her shoulder. He leaned against the frame, his hands in his pockets, surveying the room with wry amusement.

"Why? It's like a museum piece, a slice of history."

"Ouch, I'm not that old."

"How old?" she asked. She could appease a tiny segment of her curiosity.

"Twenty-nine on my next birthday. Not much older than you."

Georgia opened her mouth to refute that, then snapped it shut. Of course, he thought she was twenty-six. A narrow escape. Smiling wanly, she turned away, looking at the scraps of papers pinned to a corkboard. What had been important to Dev Tolliver as a teenager?

Dev glanced at his watch. If he knew Thelma, lunch would be waiting. Yet he didn't say anything to hurry Georgia, content to watch her prowl around his room. The thought crossed his mind he could shut the door and no one would disturb them.

Yet, despite the kisses they'd shared, he was unsure if Georgia would stand to have the door closed. She confused him and intrigued him.

Her long legs were tanned beneath her shorts. The loose top she wore might have been for camouflage, except when she moved, it clung to her body, revealing her high breasts and the gentle curve of her waist.

He remember how she'd appeared in her swimsuit in the starlight. And the growing awareness seemed all the stronger for the memory.

"Thelma will have lunch ready. Let's go," he said abruptly. He was not interested in a relationship. He had work that kept him busy. And a small circle of select friends he knew liked him for who he was, not for what he had.

"Sure. Thanks for letting me see your room. It's different from mine as a kid. My grandmother insisted it be decorated for a young girl, but I was never allowed to have a single toy out of place except when I was playing with it, or a single book not properly placed on its shelf when I finished reading. I wish I could have hung up posters," she said wistfully as she passed him.

Dev inhaled her fragrance, sweet and light—touching him deep inside like nothing else ever had. He wanted to pull her into his arms and kiss her. To feel the soft curves of her body against him as he had last night. Explore the burning attraction that grew each moment, until he could put out the flame and move on.

Georgia ran lightly down the stairs. "Thanks for the tour."

"Wait." He followed, catching up when they reached the ground level. His hand grabbed her arm, stopping her precipitous flight, swinging her around to face him.

"Where are you going?"

"To my apartment. I have an idea of the kind of flowers to make into arrangements. I'll have them ready the day your parents return. No problem. So I'm done, right?"

"Stay for lunch." Slowly the impression of her soft skin filtered to his mind. He wanted to rub his fingertips against the silky texture and absorb the sensations. Holding his impulse in check, going against his strong inclination, he released her.

"Oh, I couldn't do that."

"Thelma will have prepared enough for an army. I know her."

She seemed torn. Dev watched the expressions chase across her face and almost laughed when she reluctantly accepted. Why the reluctance? he wondered. That was part of the mystery. Sometimes she seemed to enjoy being with him, other times she looked as if she wanted to be somewhere else, anywhere else.

True to Dev's forecast, Thelma had cold chicken salad, hot rolls and tossed fruit ready for lunch— enough for everyone.

"I thought you and Georgia could eat on the patio. It's nice out and you should take advantage of the weather before it becomes too hot," she said. "Mrs. Mitton has already set a table out there."

"Oh, I thought we'd eat in here," Georgia said. Had Thelma forgotten Georgia was also an employee of the estate? She should eat with the rest of the staff. Besides, the longer she spent with Dev, the more difficult it became to remember why she was in Houston. She should be searching for information about her father, not spending the day with Dev Tolliver.

But in the end, Georgia complied.

The patio was on the side of the house by the dining room. The flagstone was swept and tidy. She'd trimmed the grass around it herself when making sweeps with the riding mower. There were hanging baskets from the lattice cover, the plants drooping in the heat. Was she supposed to water them, she thought, stricken. They looked like they were dying.

The grass and flower beds were on automatic sprinklers. She had never thought about looking for pots and planters.

After Dev left, she'd come back and see about giving them some water.

Which reminded her, when would Dev be leaving? If she wanted to get inside the house to search for anything that might establish Samuel Williams' identity, she needed free access. Which she wasn't sure she'd get with Mrs. Mitton, but knew for certain she would not get with Dev around. Didn't he have other plans for the weekend?

Lunch was delicious. Georgia wished she could have enjoyed it, but she felt edgy—too conscious of Dev sitting at her right. If she moved her leg a bit, she'd bump his knee. She felt the warmth from his leg. Trying to ignore the sensations that built, she focused on eating. Maybe she could finish quickly and escape.

"Tell me more about Georgia Brown," Dev invited. "Beyond what's on your résumé and that you have a pregnant sister living nearby who will be delivering in November."

Had she told him Margot's delivery date? She had to watch it, she didn't want to give too much away. But what was the harm? Normally she was open and friendly. She'd think nothing about telling new friends as much about her life as she could. The danger with Dev was to safely do so without revealing who she was. He seemed genuinely interested. And she admitted to being flattered. Was he as curious about her as she was about him?

"Start easy, then," he said after the silence ran on for several minutes. "What's your favorite flower?" He watched her as she scanned the yard.

"Roses," she said promptly. She had to cut him off. The longer they spent together, the more they talked, the greater the chance he'd discover her secret. And then she'd probably be out on her ear so fast she wouldn't know which end was up.

"Floribunda, tea, climbing, which?"

Staring at him, her mind went blank. What was he talking about? Roses?

"Umm, any as long as they're red," she said, taking a large bite of salad, hoping he wouldn't expect her to talk with her mouth full. How long could she stall that way? There was only so much salad left in the serving bowl, and she had already eaten a fair amount. But anything was better than running the risk of exposure.

"Tell me Dev, do you often eat with the hired help?" she said, when she could speak again, hoping to change the subject.

His gazed narrowed. "What do you mean by that?"

She waved her hand around the patio. "My grandmother would never have sat down with—" Too late. Good grief, she was absolutely no good at this undercover work.

At his sharp look, she tried to recover. "I mean, I work for you. Should you be eating with me? Should I be here?"

"Have you been reading *Jane Eyre*? I'm not some lord of the manor, Georgia. And technically, you work for my parents. I facilitated the hiring process, but that's all. Today's your day off, right?"

She nodded, taking a breath, trying to calm her roiling senses. Remembering what happened between Mr. Rochester and his hired governess, she blinked. Listening to Dev, she tried to focus, but images of last night by the pool kept interfering. He'd kissed her and she'd kissed him back. Today she'd been wary around him, trying to keep out of his way. But he'd given no indication that he wanted to touch her, kiss her, or take this tenuous interaction any further.

Except for that hot kiss, nothing in his actions had been exceptional for a man dealing with an employee.

He looked at her.

"What?" Had he been talking while her mind wandered?

"I said, I often have lunch with colleagues at work. Is this any different?"

"No, I guess not. Except we're not talking business."

"I did ask what flowers you liked."

She nodded, trying to relax. He had been perfectly reasonable. It was her own conscience that was causing the problems.

For a second, she debated taking him into her confidence. Surely by now he'd know she wasn't some gold-digger after his stepfather's money. If she could just get him to listen to her story, maybe he'd be able to answer her questions.

Then she remembered his saying Samuel Williams had never lived in Mississippi. But Dev had only known the man for the last sixteen years or so. If Sam Williams thought he was still evading a murder warrant, would he tell his young stepson? And as the years progressed, when would he say, Oh, by the way, I'm wanted on a murder charge in Mississippi?

"You intrigue me," Dev said.

Georgia looked into his eyes, startled by the words. "Me? Why?"

"Let's just say you're different from other women I see."

"You're not seeing me. We're just having lunch."

"That's what I mean. Anyone else would preen and immediately think that I was suggesting something more than lunch. You're the opposite. You try to deny there is anything between us. And I think we both know there is—something."

"Right now it's lunch between us."

He nodded. "But after last night, a woman might be excused for suspecting there's more."

"Oh, the kiss." That wonderful, sexy, heat-inducing kiss that had about knocked her off her feet.

He nodded again.

"Well, people exchange kisses all the time. It doesn't have to mean anything. Right?" She needed some confirmation here. Something that would end the daydreams that would follow if she would let herself think about that kiss more than one second at a time.

"And sometimes kissing does mean something."

"Well, sure, between a man and a woman who have a mutual attraction for each other."

"As we do not?"

Georgia shook her head, her eyes firmly fixed on her salad. This conversation was getting out of hand. She couldn't continue to deny the attraction she felt for Dev much longer. If she did, he'd begin to suspect she was protesting too much. But she couldn't let herself be sidetracked—no matter how sexy and tantalizing the distraction.

She was on a quest, and it didn't include falling for Dev Tolliver!

"Liar," he said softly, teasingly.

She looked up, shocked. Did he suspect—

No, he was flirting with her. He didn't believe her assertion that she was uninterested. Was he daring her to admit to the attraction that shimmered between them?

"I think you're too used to women throwing themselves at you," she said primly.

"Ah, the flies at my feet."

Heat flushed through her but she refused to give in

to embarrassment. "That's right. And I'm sorry to disappoint you, but I won't be one of them."

"Wanna bet?" he said softly, leaning closer. His breath fanned against her cheek, and she wanted to follow suit. Lean closer. Until their lips touched.

Heat spiraled through her as she met his gaze, held it as long as she could. The shimmering sensations that invaded every cell held her enthralled. Would another kiss hurt?

"Is that some sort of challenge?" she asked, placing her fork on her plate and sitting up straight as if prepared to do battle.

He sprawled back in his chair, stretching out his legs, brushing hers in the process. Slowly he smiled. "Could be."

Georgia jumped up, pushing back her chair. "I'm here to take care of the garden, Mr. Tolliver, not flirt with the estate owners' son." She started to turn, had a second thought and reached out to grab another of Thelma's heavenly baking powder biscuits. She stormed across the yard. Hearing Dev's mocking laughter behind her, she tossed her head and kept walking. That man was as arrogant as any of the young doctors that strutted through the halls of the hospital.

Maybe it was time he realized not every woman swooned at his feet. Though she was hard pressed to imagine anyone trying to resist. Especially herself.

It was late in the afternoon when she heard his sports car. Peering between the slats of the blinds in her window, she watched as he put down the top, and prepared to leave. Just before backing out of the long driveway, he looked up—directly into her eyes.

Only he couldn't see her, could he?

From his audacious wave, she suspected he could.

Darn! She could almost hear his laughter. And knew the point had gone to him.

It was odd to think the day had become flat, just because he'd gone out. She'd been on her own since leaving the lunch table. But it was only when he left the estate that she felt lonely. Maybe she should go up to the house and talk with Mrs. Mitton or Thelma.

Or maybe she needed to read more of the gardening book before Monday so she had some idea of how to spend her time during the coming week. If only Samuel Williams would come home early. She'd talk to him, resolve the situation one way or the other and be on her way back to New Orleans.

Late the next morning, Georgia garnered her courage and headed for the main house. She considered today was the best day to try Patrick's plan to look for clues into the history of this Samuel Williams.

Dev had not returned yesterday. Georgia ignored the pang that knowledge brought. Had he taken someone else out? Stayed the night? Not that she cared. He could do whatever he wanted.

But it had been late when she at last fell asleep. Her first action this morning had been to peek through the blinds to look for his car.

Turning away from the empty driveway, she tried to focus on her quest.

She'd tell Mrs. Mitton she needed to see the rooms

again. Hopefully the housekeeper wouldn't accompany her. Hadn't Dev vouched for her?

It was almost too easy, Georgia thought a few minutes later as she walked alone into the foyer. The warm welcome from both Mrs. Mitton and Thelma made her feel guilty about her deception. Their generous trusting natures pricked her conscience.

When she stood in the doorway to the study, however, Georgia realized she would not be able to delve into secret places. Patrick might be able to search a person's home when in the course of some investigation, but she just couldn't do it. She'd been raised by a strict woman who had definite ideas about privacy and that much, at least, had rubbed off on Georgia.

She roamed around the room, touching the desk, the chair behind it. One wall was lined with bookshelves filled with an eclectic assortment of books. She scanned the titles, touching one every so often when she recognized one she'd read. He seemed to like mysteries, as did she. Did that suggest a tie?

Sitting in one of the wing-back chairs that flanked a wide table, she wondered what Dev liked. What books he enjoyed. Did he spend a lot of time in here?

The room reflected a man's taste. There were no curtains on the windows, just wooden blinds—opened now, as were the windows, to let in the sunshine and fresh air. The room had a similar view as the sunroom, she noted, the bare patch where she'd eradicated the flowers still glaringly obvious.

Georgia didn't know how much time passed, until suddenly she heard Dev's voice. He was in the house, calling for her! Mrs. Mitton must have told him she was here.

Jumping to her feet, Georgia crossed the room silently, heading for the door. Could she get to the living room before he saw her? She had no business being in his father's office. He'd be furious if he discovered her here. And maybe suspicious.

He was already in the foyer.

Looking around frantically, she spied the window. Dashing across the room, she looked down. It wasn't a far drop into a flower bed with the soft dirt. The chances of getting hurt were minimal. Without another thought, she sat on the sill, pushed away the hinged screen, swung her legs out and jumped.

"Oof." The landing was harder than she expected. The screen slammed against the window frame, trembled a moment, then stayed in place. Dropping to her knees, she hugged the house, crouching by the wall, hoping Dev had not seen her as she dropped out of sight. Praying he'd go away long enough for her to dash across the yard and get back to her apartment.

She counted the seconds as they ticked by and nothing happened. Georgia began to relax. That was close, but at least she escaped. She leaned forward on her knees, the dirt cool and slightly damp against her skin. Crawling toward the grass, she moved slowly, quietly, cautiously.

"Georgia?"

Darn! Slowly she sank back on her feet, and looked over her shoulder at Dev. Framed in the window, he gazed back at her.

"What are you doing?"

Trying to get away from you before you suspect

more than you should, she thought, searching frantically for an answer. "I saw some, uh, weeds. *E varicose,* you know? I can't stand to have them mess up a flower garden." Slowly, using her body to shield her hand from his sight, she pulled up a plant.

Had he seen her go through the window?

"Mrs. Mitton said you'd been in the house a while ago. I called, but I guess you'd already left."

"Umm." Slowly Georgia stood, brushing the dirt from her knees. "I, uh, wanted to see the living room again to see what flowers would work. I didn't need long to do that."

"I don't expect you to work on Sundays."

"Right. I was just walking by and saw the weeds," she said, holding out the dangling plant. She hoped it wasn't some rare flower that couldn't be replaced.

"And couldn't resist?" Was there mockery in his voice?

She shrugged, stepped out of the flower bed and turned toward the garage. "I'll wait until tomorrow, then."

"Want to go to the beach?" Dev asked as Georgia took a step away.

She looked at him over her shoulder, turning slowly to face the window. "You and me?"

"In my car with the top down," he said slowly as if gauging how much of a treat she'd find it.

Wow, she'd love to drive in that sexy convertible sports car of his. And she loved the beach.

She *was* supposed to be on vacation.

But to spend the day with Dev? Could she manage that and stay sane?

Taking a deep breath, she decided she liked danger.

Smiling up at him, she drawled, "Sure thing, sugar. Let me clean up and get my suit!"

He laughed. "You almost sound like a Southern belle putting on that accent," he said.

Stricken, Georgia tried to hold onto her smile. How could she forget to disguise her voice! Using what he thought was her normal New York accent, she told him she'd meet him at the car.

She almost ran to her apartment, knowing the butterflies in her stomach were the result of living precariously. She was definitely tempting fate by spending so many hours alone with Dev.

But who could resist an invitation to the beach by a devilishly attractive man? She had had days of practice guarding her secret. She could do it for another few hours.

What she could not do was resist the chance to spend those few hours with him. Since Georgia had no way of telling what the future held, she'd grab on to today and enjoy herself.

Fifteen minutes later she closed the door to the apartment and started down the stairs. Dev leaned against the garage wall at the foot of the steps, arms crossed, as if he had all the time in the world. His khaki pants ended with bare feet slipped into Docksides. His shirt was a pale green pullover, enhancing his tan, the dark depth of his hair.

But the muscles that showed beneath the shirt drew her attention. He'd be the perfect model for the hospital's Anatomy 101 course—except no nurse in training would give a fig for the name of the muscles, they'd just want to touch him.

Tightening her hands into fists, Georgia vowed to

keep the afternoon carefree and casual. No giving in to temptation to touch that warm tanned skin to feel the heat. No skimming her fingertips over the muscles, to test the steel beneath.

"I'm ready." She almost groaned at her breathless tone.

He nodded, pushed away from the wall and took her bag. Her purse was roomy and she'd stuffed a towel inside. She wore her suit beneath her shorts and knew she could just pull on her clothes over it once she'd dried from swimming.

"This all?"

"Has my wallet inside, a towel and sunscreen. Do I need anything else?"

"You tell me, Georgia Brown." He brushed his lips across hers lightly and watched as if waiting for a reaction.

Georgia's heart skipped a beat then raced. She leaned closer, smiling up into his eyes. Slowly she licked her lips, placed one hand on his shoulder, took a deep breath that expanded her chest. Giddy with the knowledge that he'd noticed, she made her voice as sexy as possible when she said,

"Can I drive?"

CHAPTER FIVE

DEV roared with laughter. "You minx! I thought you were coming on to me."

Georgia grinned. "So, can I?"

He raised her chin with the edge of his hand and lowered his face close to hers. Two could play this game. Slowly he perused her, noting the hint of color in her cheeks, the way her blue eyes seemed to shine from within, the wispy blond hair blowing back in the gentle breeze. Then he looked at her mouth, and remembered their kiss by the pool.

"No one drives that baby but me."

She shivered and stepped back, color rising. Satisfied he'd given as good as she'd dished out, he almost smiled as she hurried to the passenger side. For a moment he'd thought she—

Better let that go. He was not looking for any kind of entanglement. A fun afternoon at the beach. That was all.

"It was worth a try," she said when he opened the door for her.

In only seconds, the top was down and the engine on. Buckling her seat belt, Georgia leaned back, prepared to enjoy herself. The wind in her hair moments later felt wonderful, blowing away the doubts about what she was trying to do.

When she returned later, she'd have to call her sisters. She'd tell Margot she was enjoying her vacation.

But when she reached Shelby, she'd find out if Patrick had discovered anything else about the men they were researching.

For now, however, she gave herself up to the beauty of the day—and the excitement of spending it with Dev.

"How close is the beach to Houston?" she asked.

"We'll drive to Galveston. I had Thelma pack a quick lunch for us. Want to listen to the radio? Since you worked in New Orleans, I bet you like jazz."

She nodded.

Dev tuned in an all-jazz station. With the sound of the wind whipping by their ears and the other cars on the highway, conversation was difficult. Georgia didn't even try.

When they reached Galveston, Dev drove confidently through town, obviously knowing his way around. Soon he pulled into the driveway of a large home overlooking the Gulf.

"Is this your place?" Georgia asked, sitting up. The house was lovely, built of natural cedar with lots of glass on the water side.

"No, it belongs to a friend of my mother's. Since the family lives in Dallas most of the year, we check up on the place for them every so often. The seashore here is quiet, there won't be many people around."

The beach was lovely, Georgia thought, as she walked beside Dev a few minutes later on the pristine white sand. Wide and clean, it seemed to go on forever. Here and there family groups enjoyed the water. Little children built sand castles in the damp sand. Mothers sat beneath umbrellas watching and reading.

The crowds usually found at public beaches were missing.

"This is wonderful," Georgia said, dropping down beside Dev after he spread a blanket and placed the picnic basket on one corner.

"Want to swim first and then eat?"

"Sure." She slipped out of her shorts, pulled her shirt over her head. Looking at Dev, she felt suddenly shy though her one-piece teal blue bathing suit was not daring.

His expression showed pure male interest. Feeling deliciously feminine, she dropped her shirt and turned for the water, conscious of his gaze touching every inch of her. She wanted to return that perusal, but couldn't bring herself to do it.

Splashing into the warm water, she ducked beneath a shallow wave and struck out swimming hard. In no time Dev was right beside her. She should have expected it after seeing all those swimming trophies in his bedroom.

When she was pleasantly tired, she turned over to float. The sky was a cloudless blue, deep and endless. The water felt cool enough to be refreshing, yet warm enough to enjoy without getting chilled.

Dev stopped swimming when she did, lazily treading water beside her as he studied the shoreline, the houses in the background.

"This is nice," Georgia said, coming upright and paddling.

"Every summer Houston becomes hot and humid, so coming to the Gulf is necessary to survival. When I was a kid, we used to come and stay with the

Stanyons for weeks on end. My dad likes the Gulf—he used to work on some of the rigs off the coast.''

Georgia went still. Her father had also worked the rigs in the Gulf. Hadn't Edith Strong told Patrick and Shelby that he'd worked on the ones near the mouth of the Mississippi River?

"Where?" she asked casually, her heart beating faster.

"Near Brownsville. Ever seen an oil rig?"

"Only pictures."

"Once every five years they gave tours to the families of the men who work on them. I remember going right after Samuel married my mother. It wasn't long after that when he moved up in the company and began buying shares until he eventually obtained controlling interest."

"Your father owns the oil company?" Georgia said in shock. She knew from his lavish home that the Texas contender for the Beaufort girls' father had money, but she hadn't realized how much.

"It's only a regional oil company, not British Petroleum," Dev said, his eyes studying her.

Georgia nodded in a daze and began to swim back to the beach. No wonder Dev was wary on his father's behalf. With that much money behind him, he was probably used to people trying to get something for nothing.

When Georgia waded out of the water, she debated the advisability of contacting Patrick and reassessing her plan. He had mentioned nothing about Samuel Williams owning controlling interest in an oil company. Surely he knew it. Why let her come into this without that information?

Her plan had seemed so easy when she'd proposed it. Now that she'd met Dev and learned more about his stepfather, she wasn't so sure. Would the man, even if he was her father, suspect she had only sought to find him because of money?

Would Dev?

Trying to shake an odd premonition, Georgia sat on the blanket and opened the picnic basket. She'd have to think this through, but later, when she was alone. Right now she had to make sure Dev suspected nothing.

"Wow, Thelma outdid herself. This is a quick lunch?" she asked as she began to unpack the basket. To her surprise, there were real china plates. She opened some of the containers, finding thin slices of ham and roast beef, mustard, fresh croissants, cold vegetables with a tangy sauce for dipping. For dessert, sugar-sprinkled strawberries.

"What a feast!"

Dev lay down on his side, propped up on his elbow watching Georgia select from each container, filling their plates. Her enthusiasm was contagious. He reached out for his dark glasses and pulled them on. Watching her reminded him of days gone by. When he'd been a teenager and everything had been easy and fun.

As an adult, especially lately, he viewed things more cynically. What other woman of his acquaintance would be so delighted with the simple fare Thelma had prepared on such short notice?

Briefly his thoughts flashed to his onetime fiancée, Elizabeth. She had shown only disdain for picnics. Her preference had always been for high-priced restaurants where she could be seen. One of her dresses probably cost more than everything he'd seen Georgia wear, and then some.

He frowned. He didn't want to think about Elizabeth, or what a fool he'd made of himself over her.

"Don't you like this?" Georgia said, offering one of the laden plates.

"Yeah." Dev sat up and reached for the plate.

"So why the frown?"

"Just thinking of someone else."

"Oh? A girlfriend? Probably wishing she was here instead of me."

He looked at her sharply. She didn't seem put out by the thought. And for some reason, that irritated him.

"I don't wish she was here. Elizabeth was nothing but trouble. And nothing like you." He bit down savagely on the croissant, ignoring the way it almost melted on his tongue.

"How are we different?" Georgia began eating, enjoying her food, obviously delighting in everything about the outing, from the beach, to the water, to the picnic lunch.

"For one thing, she never showed any of the enthusiasm that you do. Hasn't the novelty of things worn a bit thin?" he asked sarcastically.

"Nope. I think this place is enchanting. I'm having a great time despite your surly mood. If you don't want to think of Elizabeth, why do it?"

"It pays to remember life's mistakes so they aren't repeated."

"And what life lesson did she teach?"

"Never get involved with anyone whose bank account isn't at least equal to my father's!"

He looked away from her stunned expression. Time she knew the facts of life. He was attracted to her. Enjoyed spending time with her. But that was as far as he was willing to go. It had nothing to do with lord of the manor and an employee, but more with the knowledge that without an equal bank balance, he'd never know for sure a woman wanted him for himself and not his money.

"Define get involved," she said, scooting around on the sand.

He glanced back. She'd put down her plate and was watching him steadily from grave blue eyes.

"Get serious about a woman."

"That sure limits the gene pool." She picked up a sliver of ham and popped it into her mouth.

"What do you mean?"

"If your father owns an oil company, he's probably obscenely rich. Which means there are not going to be a lot of women your age sitting around on an equal pile of money. And the chances of meeting those who do are slim, therefore your choice is going to be very limited."

Dev watched her finish her roll and wipe the plate with a napkin. When she looked at him it was with a considerable effort that he didn't question her further.

"I'm going for a walk," she said, pulling on her own dark glasses and standing to head down the beach.

Déjà vu. Hadn't she walked away from their lunch yesterday?

He rose in one smooth movement and joined her by the water's edge.

"You didn't finish your lunch. Thelma will be unhappy if you don't eat the strawberries."

"I'll snack on the ride home," she said, her head held high. "You go eat your share now if you want."

"I'll walk with you," he said, matching his stride with hers.

"Don't bother. Someone might suspect you are becoming involved and I got that message loud and clear."

He detected the hurt underlying her voice. For some reason he wanted to purge it. True, he had been warning her off, but he hadn't meant to hurt her feelings. They'd spent a few hours together over the last few days. That was all.

Except for those kisses.

But that kind of thing meant nothing. It was kindest to let her know up front he was not in any matrimonial stakes.

Not that she had shown a lot of interest so far in this relationship.

Relationship? No, two people spending a few hours at the beach did *not* constitute a relationship.

"You'll get sunburned," he said as he glanced at her bare shoulders. Her skin was fair, lightly tanned, but the sun and water were a brutal combination. He didn't want her to burn.

He didn't want anything to hurt her, he realized. Including himself. Her sunny disposition was a refreshing experience. He hoped nothing would ever happen to change that for Georgia.

She reversed directions and walked quickly back to

the blanket. Dev stood watching her. Would she put on sunscreen and head out in the opposite direction to avoid him?

She snatched up her shirt and the bottle of sunscreen and stomped back toward him. Dev was conscious of an easing of his muscles. She was going to continue their walk, even after he'd practically insulted her.

"If you don't mind, would you put some on my back?" she asked frostily, holding out the bottle of lotion.

"If you'll return the favor."

She nodded once and turned around.

Dev opened the cap, poured some of the warm lotion in his palm. Amazing, he thought, in twenty-eight years of living, I've never done this before. Slowly he reached out and touched her. Her skin was hot beneath his fingertips, silky soft and smooth. He spread the cream across her back, lingering as he registered the rigid tenseness of her muscles, the delicate bones of her neck and spine. Long after the lotion disappeared, he continued to caress her.

He wanted to turn her around and enfold her in his arms. See if they could share another kiss as hot as the one by the pool. See if—

"Aren't you finished yet?" She stepped aside and turned back, throwing her shirt over her shoulders. Refusing to meet his eyes, she held out the hand for the sunscreen. "Turn around and I'll do you."

Dev presented his back, gazing over the cool water, wondering if he should just plunge in before he embarrassed both of them with his body's reaction to her touch. Her palms felt firm and competent as she slathered lotion across his back. Closing his eyes for a second, Dev imagined her reaching around to rub some of that lotion on his chest. He could turn in the circle of her arms, and let her coat every inch of exposed skin. The feel of her hands fostered images that he hadn't had in a long time.

Lightly slapping his back, Georgia said, ''You're done.''

He turned slightly, to watch her spread the lotion over her long legs, wishing she'd asked him to do that too. Again images flooded his mind, of his hands rubbing over her legs, and then moving up, over her hips to caress her breasts and then holding her for a deep kiss.

Had the sun addled his brains? He was not interested in getting involved. He had made sure she got that message. Hadn't he been paying attention himself?

Georgia started to walk. Dev debated accompanying her. He'd laid out the ground rules, so there'd be no harm in enjoying the afternoon together.

When he joined her, she glanced at him, and he wished she had not put on her dark glasses. Her face was expressionless. What was she thinking?

''Tell me about going to the beach as a child. Did you build sand castles? Practice swimming? Were you ever here during a hurricane?'' she asked as they strolled along. The water brushed across their feet, receded.

''You seem to have a curious fixation on hearing about my past,'' Dev said lightly, wondering why all their conversations seemed to start there.

''It's because I didn't have parents, so I like listening to someone who did. Don't tell me if you don't want."

"I don't mind. But I suspect you already know more about my past than close friends I've had for years. By the time my mother married Samuel, I was too old to build sand castles. And he was the one who brought us to the beach."

"Ha, no one is too old. You just thought you were because you were probably some bratty teenager who thought he was hot stuff."

"Well, that cuts me down to size."

"As if anything could. So if you didn't make sand castles, what did you do?"

"Swimming. Some underwater stuff. The Stanyons have a speedboat over at the marina, so we'd go water-skiing, or just take off for the fun of it."

"What does your father look like?" she asked.

"Why?"

"I'm, um, trying to envision the two of you in a boat and can't picture him."

"He's tall. Had thick brown hair when he married Mom, now it's getting a bit gray, but is still thick. His skin is dark—from spending so much time in the sun on the oil rigs, I guess." Dev looked at her. She constantly surprised him. "So now you can picture him and me on a boat?"

She shrugged. "What's your mom like?"

"She's not very tall. She works at keeping gray from her hair. It's sort of a light brown. She still has a nice figure. And is very active, always working for some charity event or the other. Samuel's been good for her. She had a hard time with her first husband."

"It's nice, I guess, that they both found happiness

the second time around,'' Georgia said slowly as she thought about the past. Once her mother had died, there was no reason for her father not to remarry. Only—the thought just occurred. How had he known he was free?

"It's not Dad's second marriage," Dev said shortly. "You asked that once and I told you he hadn't been married before. Why do you think he was?"

She looked at him, annoyed with the slip. Dev was too smart to not pick up on everything.

"I don't. I don't know anything about him. I meant it was nice that they both found happiness and it's your mother's second time." She spun around and headed for the blanket. "It's getting late. I need to get back. There are things I need to do." She picked up the pace.

The afternoon was proving to be a strain. Despite Dev's warning, she couldn't help thinking how easily she responded around him. He was intelligent and attentive and could turn a woman's head in a second if she weren't careful. But he'd been clear he wanted nothing permanent. And once he found out her true reason for being in Texas, he'd probably raise the roof.

"What's so important on a Sunday afternoon that you have to cut this short to get back for?" he asked, keeping stride with her every step.

"Just things." When she reached the blanket, she pulled on her shorts, buttoned her shirt. "Besides, I don't want to take up all your day, you might suspect some misguided attempt on my part to get involved with you."

Dev shook his head. "You wouldn't even be in the running."

Annoyed afresh at how much his words stung, Georgia hastily repacked the lunch things, and walked up toward the house, and the car in the driveway. There had already been a strong reason to stay away from Dev. He'd just given her another.

Georgia was silent on the ride home. She wondered if there was any way to prove the Houston Sam Williams was her father without having to wait for him to return. Dev hadn't said a word to her once they'd reached the car. She hoped he wasn't rehashing their conversation. Was he beginning to suspect?

Heaven help her if he did. With the tenacity he'd shown thus far, once he had a glimmer, she wouldn't stand a chance to keep the truth from him. And she still had nearly a week to go! Another six days before she could talk to the man she'd come to see.

Another six days of seeing Dev?

She let her gaze drift over to him. Involuntarily she recalled the feel of his warm skin beneath her hands when she spread the sunscreen. Tightening her fingers into a fist, she tried to ignore the clamoring of her senses to touch again. To feel the strength, the substance of the man.

In seeking information about the father, she was learning about the son. She wanted to learn even more. Yet, why? There was no future for them. She only had a couple of weeks left of her vacation. Hopefully she could discover if Samuel Williams was her father. But in any case, when her time was up, she had to return to New Orleans, to her new job in the

Trauma Unit at the hospital, and resume her normal life.

New Orleans seemed a long way from Houston.

When Dev pulled into the long driveway, he drove straight to the garage. He shut off the engine and leaned back, looking at Georgia.

"Thanks for a nice afternoon," she said.

He laughed, shaking his head. "Ever polite. Your grandmother would be proud."

"I doubt it," she mumbled, gathering her oversized purse and preparing to get out of the car. It was more likely her grandmother would be spinning in her grave to know Georgia was impersonating a gardener!

"Have dinner with me."

"What?" She looked at him in surprise. After the silent treatment all the way home, after his insistence he was not looking for any involvement, the last thing she expected was an invitation to spend more time with him.

"I don't think so." She opened the door and stepped out. Closing it, she let her hand pat the car one last time. Riding in a convertible had been fun. "See ya." Before she could change her mind, she ran lightly up the stairs to her apartment.

The man was driving her nuts. Coming on to her with one hand, and then slapping her away with the other. Sighing, she pushed away from the door. She'd take a quick shower, fix some soup for dinner and call her sisters.

Resigned to either giving up her quest or playing the role of gardener for another few days, Georgia decided to avoid any serious changes to the estate gardens but to give the appearance from a distance of working. She hoped Mrs. Mitton and Thelma hadn't a clue about what was supposed to go on in the yard.

"I'll treat it as in medicine—first do no harm," she mumbled as she walked around one of the flowerbeds Monday morning. Though when she glanced around the entire yard her courage almost failed. Even an outsider could see the neglect. Trimming the dead blossoms from the stalks was only a first step. If the plants looked odd or lopsided, she cut the stalks nearer the ground. If she totally ruined something, she'd just have to replace it.

Expecting to be left alone during the week, Georgia was surprised at the warm invitation to join them for meals that she received from Mrs. Mitton and Thelma. They insisted she eat lunch and dinner with them, regaling her with tales of places they'd worked. They fussed over her, tempting her with delicacies that Thelma loved to bake. Georgia enjoyed herself more than she'd expected.

Dev continued to work long hours. Twice during the week, Georgia was already in bed when she heard his car. The other nights, it had taken all her resolve to stay behind closed doors when he arrived home.

After the first dinner, Georgia realized she had a gold mine of information ready to be tapped in the two long-time employees. When she had casually asked how long they'd worked for the Williamses, she'd been delighted to learn both had been with them for a number of years.

"Nicest folks around. I remember when Dev was just a young teenager, couldn't get enough of my cookies," Thelma said, smiling broadly. "Even now,

he always swings by the kitchen when he visits to see
if I made a fresh batch.''

"Well, I remember how much trouble it was to get
him to put his clothes in the hamper," Mrs. Mitton
countered, but the twinkle in her eye left Georgia with
the feeling the housekeeper hadn't minded a bit. The
man was definitely spoiled by the females in his life.

Georgia giggled. Hard to believe the rugged businessman was once a typical teenager. Wouldn't he be
frustrated to hear that being shared!

"Tell me more. Does Mr. Williams share Dev's
love of cookies?"

"He does have a sweet tooth. But he prefers cakes.
Mrs. Williams, now, she loves fresh salads and vegetables. Thin as a rail, I say, but she doesn't eat the
desserts like her men.''

It occurred to Georgia as she listened to the stories
the women told that she was learning a lot about Dev.
None of which would matter if this Samuel Williams
didn't turn out to be *her* father. Nevertheless, she
learned more and more, and continued to ply the
women with questions.

Thursday evening, Georgia showered and donned a
pair of light-blue shorts and a short matching crop
top. It had been hot and humid all day and she was
glad it was drawing to an end. After the rest of the
staff retired, she planned to sneak back to the pool
and indulge herself in another midnight swim. She
hoped Dev came home early enough to be asleep by
the time she made her clandestine swim.

She slipped on sandals and headed for the main

house, hoping Thelma had prepared another one of her salads. It was too hot to eat a heavy meal.

Stepping inside, she noticed immediately that the big kitchen table had only two places set.

"Is Mrs. Mitton not eating with us tonight?" she asked. The air-conditioned room felt heavenly against her heated skin.

Thelma looked up and smiled. "There you are. I set your place on the patio tonight."

"With mine," Dev said, from the doorway between the kitchen and the dining room.

Georgia swung around, surprised to see him. "Hi. I didn't know you were here." Had she missed seeing his car in the driveway?

Her heart rate increased slightly and she felt a flush of warmth that the air conditioner couldn't cool at the sight of him. She hadn't seen him since Sunday afternoon. She refused to admit she'd missed him!

She looked at Thelma. "I thought I'd eat in here with you and Mrs. Mitton."

"Oh, go on with you. Dev'd like company for dinner, someone his own age. I've set the table in the shade on the patio. It's cooling off. You two young people have more to discuss than listening to stories Mrs. Mitton and I have to tell."

Dev folded his arms across his chest and leaned casually against the jamb, but Georgia wasn't fooled. He was as alert as ever. As he glanced from Thelma to her, she could almost see the speculation rising. Hoping to forestall any questions on his part about what stories she'd been told, she plunged into speech.

"I don't think I should be eating with him. I like eating in here with you."

"She thinks of me as lord of the manor," Dev said. His tone was light, his gaze never leaving Georgia's.

Thelma laughed. "That'll be the day that a Texan puts on airs. Go on with you, I'll bring out dinner in a bit. There's already a pitcher of iced tea and some rolls on the table." Making a shooing motion, she urged them from the kitchen.

"I can get something on my own," Georgia murmured as she reluctantly followed Dev through the house and onto the patio.

"And spoil Thelma's matchmaking scheme?"

Her gaze flew to his. "You're not serious?"

Dev encircled her neck with one hand, pulling her close enough that she could feel the heat from his body envelope her. Lowering his head, he rested his forehead on hers, his eyes looking deep into Georgia's.

"Oh, yes, Georgia Brown. I'm serious. We like each other—that's the whole problem."

Swallowing hard, she blinked, mesmerized by the desire evident in his eyes.

"But you said you weren't going to become involved with someone like me."

He didn't say a word, merely covered her mouth with his and kissed her.

The world spun and Georgia grabbed on to keep from spinning with it. Before she realized it, her arms encircled his neck, and she returned his kiss, reveling in the sensations that swept through her. His tongue sought entry and she parted her lips to enjoy the new sweep of impressions that clamored for expression.

A sound from the house alerted them, and Dev quickly released her and stepped away. In only a second, Thelma bustled out, carrying a heavily laden tray.

"We'll continue this discussion later," Dev said.

Some discussion, Georgia thought, as she moved in a daze to take one of the chairs. Her heart beat rapidly in her chest, her skin felt even hotter than before, and there was definitely something wrong with her breathing.

What was there to discuss? She was afraid she was falling for the man, and he had already firmly posted No Trespassing signs!

CHAPTER SIX

"HARD week?" he asked when Thelma left.

"No. How about you?" Georgia tried to smother her guilty feelings. Reading the gardening book had served to provide her enough information to feel confident in the minimal work she was doing. At least she didn't think she was ruining any plants. The yard was more than she could handle as anyone would see if they looked closely. But she only needed a couple of more days.

She served the salads Thelma had made—a German potato salad and a tasty tuna salad. She sipped her tea and then began to eat, conscious of Dev sitting only a few feet from her. She wanted to look at him, but was too afraid of what her eyes might reveal.

"My week was not hard as much as hectic and long. I'll be glad when Dad's back at the helm," Dev said as he began to eat.

"Is he well enough to return right away?"

"Not full-time immediately. But he'll be able to come in for a few hours every day."

"I'd think you'd love the chance to run the company," she said. She suspected he'd be good at it.

"It's challenging and exciting. And Dad plans for me to take over when he retires. But not yet. He's only in his fifties. Besides, the difference would be once I was in complete charge, I'd hire someone to replace me.''

"So you're really doing two jobs."

He nodded.

"What's involved in running an oil company?" Maybe she could get him talking, and avoid any awkward questions.

"No you don't. I've noticed every time we're together, you ask questions. Tonight it's your turn to give me some answers."

Georgia went still. "What answers?"

She met his gaze, hoping she hid the trepidation his words brought.

"You could start with telling me how you ended up specializing in gardening. Or how does the climate and the soil here differ from what you were used to dealing with in Louisiana and New York. Or, how you feel about becoming an aunt."

Smiling spontaneously at the last, she said, "I love the thought of becoming an aunt again. You know that Margot was pregnant a long time ago and miscarried. This is her second attempt and we're all tiptoing around her to make sure nothing gets her upset. Not that stress was identified as the cause last time, but we're taking no chances."

"Becoming an aunt again? You're already an aunt?"

"By marriage. My sister Shelby married a man who has a four-year-old daughter. We hit it off instantly. She's adorable."

"You like kids?"

"I'm not around any on a regular basis. But Mollie

is precious. And I expect to be asked to baby-sit a lot when Margot's baby arrives.''

''That's why you moved here, right? To be near your sister.''

Georgia held her breath. That had been the cover story. Slowly she nodded. ''I want to be near Margot and watch her baby grow, to be a part of his or her life from the beginning.'' Stick to the truth as much as possible, she thought.

Dev finished his meal and pushed the plate aside, settling back in his chair. ''I'm surprised you aren't married.''

''Good grief, I'm just starting out. It's too soon to get married.''

''Most women on the far side of twenty-five think time's running out.''

Oops, she'd forgotten she was supposed to be older.

''You're not married. And you're on that far side.''

He nodded, his expression closing. ''I almost married once.''

''What happened?''

''It's ancient history now.''

''But the reason you want no involvements with women, right?'' she guessed shrewdly.

''Right. If you're finished, we could move to the pool area. The chairs there are more comfortable.''

Georgia recognized a closed subject when she heard it. But her curiosity rose another notch. What had happened to make him so cynical about women? Obviously it had to do with his former fiancée, but what specifically?

If she was at all prudent, she'd make some excuse

and head for her apartment. Dinner was over, the ordeal safely survived.

But she'd missed him during the week. Missed hearing his voice, listening to him talk. She could be on guard, watch every word, and take the chance to spend a little more time with him. It was already Thursday. If all went according to plan, by Saturday she'd know the truth about Samuel Williams and be on her way back to New Orleans.

What could one more evening with Dev hurt?

He pulled two lounge chairs into the shade, facing the pool. He eased down on one and leaned back. Gingerly, Georgia slipped into the chair next to his. It was still hot, but not unbearably so in the shade. And once the sun went down, it would become cooler. The pool looked inviting. Dare she hope he might want to go swimming later?

"What kinds of books do you read?" he asked, once she was settled. "What movies do you like? I know you like jazz, do you like other kinds of music?"

"Bluegrass," she said. "We used to hear it on the riverboats as they made their way upriver when they'd pass Beau—" Stopping suddenly she realized she'd almost given Beaufort Hall as her home. It wouldn't take him two seconds to make the connection to the Miss Beaufort who had tried to reach his father. Besides, she was supposed to be from New York.

"Pass where?"

"Uh, Beauregard Point, just outside New Orleans. What kind of music do *you* like?"

"I thought you were from New York," he said slowly.

Yikes! "Um, I am. But we came to visit a cousin who lived in New Orleans. That's why I went there when I was starting out. Always liked it. Anyway, that was ages ago. What's your favorite music?"

She needed to get off the topic of her life. Maybe Patrick could think quickly when on an undercover assignment, but she found it full of unexpected traps.

"Some rock, and of course country and western. You can't live in Texas and not like country-western music."

Georgia smiled.

"Tell me your favorite memory as a child," Dev said.

"My favorite memory? Why?"

"I've shared escapades of my youth with you," he said easily. "Turnabout's fair play."

"Careful, Mr. Tolliver, you sound almost interested."

"And is that a crime?"

"Only if it leads to involvement." Georgia knew she skated near the edge, but she couldn't help it.

"Which won't happen. Tell me something, Georgia."

"Okay. Let's see. How about the time Bobby Benton and I made a tree fort and played cowboys and Indians for days!"

"How old were you?"

"Twelve." Just before her grandmother began harping on her becoming a lady suitable enough to deserve the Beaufort name.

She launched into the story, embellishing for effect,

recalling the sense of freedom she'd felt as they made the fort just the way they wanted, trying to make the scene come alive for Dev. When she finished, she looked over and blinked.

The man had fallen asleep.

Torn between amusement and a sudden feeling of protectiveness, she watched him. His eyelashes made a dark crescent against his tanned skin. Even in sleep, his appeal held. She knew he was tired. And from what he'd said earlier, doing two jobs meant spending long hours at the office every day. She felt an odd sense of contentment that Dev felt comfortable enough around her to completely relax.

Slowly Georgia rose and stepped away. She'd let him sleep. He obviously needed that more than companionship.

It was after ten when he knocked on her door. Opening it, Georgia grinned up at him. "Next time I'll just stick to the old fairy tales. I understand they're great for putting children to sleep."

"You should have woken me," he said, resting one arm against the door jamb. "Want to go swimming?"

"I thought about it earlier, but now that I've been ensconced in this air-conditioned apartment for a few hours, I don't think so. In fact, I was getting ready to go to bed."

He hesitated a moment, then shrugged, straightening away from the door, looking over the grounds.

"Tomorrow night I have to attend a party one of our customers is giving. It'll be in a hotel downtown. Would you come with me?" He turned back and looked her full in the face.

"Tomorrow night? Why Dev, honey, this is so sudden.'' Batting her eyelashes, she did her best rendition of a Southern belle.

"Flirting can get you in trouble," he said, running a finger down her cheek.

Georgia shivered, feeling his touch to her toes. Just how much trouble?

"It's not much notice," she said, stalling, amazed to discover how strongly she wanted to go.

"I was planning to attend alone, but thought you might like to go. Make up for my falling asleep on your favorite memory."

"Not necessary. Besides, I work for you."

"For my parents. You sure have a hang-up about that. What if you were a gardener for the next-door neighbors, would you still feel the same about seeing me?"

"Maybe not." But that would never happen. Unless another Samuel Williams moved in next door, she thought whimsically.

"I'll pick you up at seven. It's dressy."

"Then I can truthfully say I don't have anything to wear."

"When are your clothes coming? I thought they'd be here by now."

"Soon. I guess I could quit a bit early tomorrow and see about buying a new dress. I'll make up the time on Saturday."

"I don't think a couple of hours off would hurt anything. See you tomorrow."

For a moment Georgia thought he'd kiss her, but he just looked at her for a long moment, then left.

"Another major mistake. What does a twenty-two year old nurse have in common with people in the oil industry who will be at that thing tomorrow night?" she asked herself as she shut the door.

"Doesn't matter, I'll be with Dev. And that's enough!" she answered herself, smiling dreamily.

Promptly at seven the next evening, Dev knocked on her door. Georgia had spent the afternoon finding just the right dress. It was a pale blue, with spaghetti straps, a fitted bodice and a swirling skirt. Short and sassy, it fit like a dream. Peering into the mirror, she was pleased to notice the dress made her eyes seem even brighter. Her hair had picked up highlights from her hours in the sun and was glossy and shining.

Maybe she should consider taking up gardening as a hobby. Not that she had a garden at her apartment. But there was always Margot's house and Shelby's and both had large yards. It would be a shame to waste all the knowledge she was gaining.

"Wow," Georgia said when she opened the door. Dev looked fantastic! He wore a black dinner jacket, with a pristine white pleated shirt. Tall, dark and handsome sprang to mind. Followed immediately by *sexy as sin.*

"I can see we won't be discussing much business at this event. Once everyone sees you, they'll be otherwise occupied," he returned.

She smiled at the compliment. "The dress is all right, isn't it?"

"More than all right. It's perfect. You look beautiful."

Warmed by his compliment, by the look in his eyes, she knew she would enjoy the evening—as long as she kept her wits about her and revealed nothing!

"Since you bought the dress especially for this event, maybe I should reimburse you," Dev said as they began to descend the stairs.

She laughed and shook her head, touched he'd even think to offer. "Men don't buy women's clothes—unless they're married. Besides, I can always wear this at the hospital Christmas ball—" Oops. So much for revealing nothing.

"The hospital?" he asked, opening the passenger door to his car. Tonight the top was up.

"Um, the hospital near where I used to live has a charity event every Christmas. I usually go. To support them and all," she trailed off. Darn it, she was not used to this subterfuge.

"But that's in New Orleans, and you'll be here this Christmas, won't you?"

"I might go there to visit…friends." How could a person working undercover ever keep everything straight, she wondered. "Tell me about the party. I suspect it'll be huge if it's being held at a hotel ballroom."

"Titan Brothers is a major trucking firm with offices all over the state and Oklahoma. They buy their petroleum products exclusively from us. As well as provide transportation to many of the major businesses here in Texas. Every August they throw a big party and invite everyone they know. Jim-Bob Titan is the CEO. His wife, Lily, uses the event as an excuse to buy new clothes, and jewelry, to show off to the world."

"Umm. Do you go every year?"

"Usually. My folks always attend. Jim-Bob and

Dad go back a long way. This will be the first year my parents have missed.''

When they arrived at the hotel, Georgia was re-minded of the glittering charity events she attended with her grandmother in Natchez. Because of her grandmother's training, she was able to converse confidently, knowing when to be serious, and when to be amusing. Flirting a little with the older men, and keeping a distance from the younger, she enjoyed herself.

But the dancing was the best part.

Being held in Dev's arms, twirling around the floor, watching other couples swaying to the music was heavenly.

''I thought you'd do the Texas Two-Step,'' she murmured as another waltz began.

Dev smiled at her. ''Not at such a fancy event. But we can hunt up a place another night and give it a whirl if you like.''

Georgia felt her bones melt at the sight of his smile. Glad she had his shoulder and hand to hold her up, she nodded, looking away before she did something silly like move closer and give him an indication about how she felt.

Not that she wanted to examine those feelings closely. The night was young, and she didn't want introspection to interfere with having a good time.

They nibbled from the sumptuous buffet tables, sipped wine from the lavish bar. Names swirled around and around as she tried to remember everyone Dev introduced to her.

There were odd speculative glances thrown her

way. After one, Georgia looked down at her dress, down to her shoes.

"Is there something wrong with me?" she asked, looking back at Dev.

"What do you mean?"

"People keep giving us odd looks. Did I spill something on my dress?"

He scanned her from head to toe. "There's nothing on your dress."

"Then why—"

He shrugged, sipping the wine. "Probably because I haven't brought a date in years."

"Oh." Oddly pleased, she suddenly wondered why. It was just a casual date. Nothing to read into it.

"Hello, Dev." A tall man stopped in front of Dev and shook hands.

"Tyler."

"And this is?" Tyler asked as he smiled at Georgia.

"Georgia Brown," Dev said, offering nothing more.

"Would you care to dance, Georgia Brown?" Tyler asked, holding out his hand.

"I came with Dev." She looked at him.

"Dance with him if you want," Dev said carelessly.

Georgia hesitated, then smiled and shook her head. "Thanks anyway. I'll just sit this one out with Dev."

Tyler looked nonplussed. "Something going on here I should know about?" he asked.

Dev regarded Georgia, his eyes narrowed slightly.

"Nothing's going on. But you heard the lady, she doesn't want to dance."

Tyler murmured something polite and moved on.

"What was that about?" Dev asked. "Most women would love to dance with Tyler. Be seen, admired."

Georgia blinked. "First of all, I have no interest in Tyler whatever-his-last-name was. I didn't come here to be seen or admired. You invited me. I thought you wanted to spend time with me. I wanted to spend time with you. Why would I want to cut that short by dancing with someone else?"

"Why indeed," Dev said, taken with her explanation. Taking her glass, he put his and hers on the bar and drew her to the dance floor. Gathering her close, they moved in time to the tempo.

Since that first day, he'd felt something different about Georgia Brown. And trying to figure out what it was occupied more time than it should.

But he wasn't sorry she'd refused Tyler. Puzzled by it, definitely. Elizabeth would have been off in a shot. She loved to attend events where she could be the belle of the ball, loved to be the center of attention. And pouted if she didn't have her own way.

Tightening his hold on Georgia, Dev stopped thinking about the other woman and concentrated on the one in his arms. She was soft and sweet, with a sensuality that he suspected she didn't recognize. Her scent surrounded them, enhanced by the warmth of her skin. He liked it. It wasn't cloying like some women wore, but light and fragrant.

In fact, he found he liked a lot about Georgia Brown. But that's as far as he was willing to go. He'd been burned once and didn't plan to repeat the experience.

They circled the floor and Dev realized neither of them had spoken a word since beginning the dance. Other women seemed to feel duty-bound to chat incessantly when dancing. With Georgia, they both could enjoy the music, and each other.

To his surprise, he realized he was enjoying the dance—and the woman in his arms.

When the song ended, Jim-Bob Titan clapped Dev on the back.

"Hello, boy. Saw you earlier, but with this crush, I couldn't get over to talk to you before now. How're you doing? How's your dad? I heard he's doing better."

"Hello, Jim-Bob. Dad's recovering. He and Mom will be home tomorrow. The ship docked in New Orleans this afternoon. They're flying home in the morning."

"Well, you tell him hey for me and Lily. Now who's this lovely lady with you? Haven't seen you bring a date to this event in years. Not since that skinny gal you were tangled up with."

"This is Georgia Brown. Georgia, Jim-Bob Titan, our host."

"Nice to meet you, sir."

"Yessirree bob, I like this one, Dev. Got manners and looks. Glad you came, pretty lady. You having a good time?"

"I surely am, Mr. Titan."

"Jim-Bob, honey. Just Jim-Bob. I've known this boy since he was a youngster. If he gives you any trouble, you come tell old Jim-Bob."

Georgia smiled and nodded. "I'll keep that in mind."

"I'm trembling in my shoes," Dev said, his eyes twinkling.

Jim-Bob laughed, clapped him on the shoulder again. "That'll be the day. There hasn't been anyone to do anything with you since you grew up. I know your daddy's proud of you. I heard you've been keeping the company going in his absence. From a customer's point of view, you're doing fine."

Dev nodded. "I appreciate that, Jim-Bob."

"Yessirree bob, your daddy has some big shoes to fill, but you can do it. Won't have to for a few years, though, right?"

"Right. He'll be back in no time."

"See that this pretty lady enjoys herself, you hear me?"

Dev nodded again, shaking hands with the older man.

"Whew," Georgia said when Jim-Bob had moved on to greet another guest. "He has a lot of energy, doesn't he? I like him—but I bet his wife has her hands full with him!"

"Lily can handle him. And he dotes on her."

Georgia smiled a bit wistfully, wondering if anyone would ever dote on her.

It was late by the time they left even though the revelry continued. Georgia enjoyed the quiet ride home, talking about the event, basking in the contentment the evening had brought. She'd had a wonderful time.

"Thanks for inviting me. Who was that skinny woman you brought last?" she couldn't resist asking.

"Elizabeth—my ex-fiancée."

"Ah, the one who made you swear off women forever."

"Got it in one," he said as he pulled the car into the driveway and stopped at the base of the apartment stairs. Switching off the engine, he looked at her.

"You know what I think?" Georgia said, unfastening her seat belt.

"I suspect you're going to tell me."

She leaned close. "I don't think you've looked into the mirror lately. You've got so much going for you that it would be a pity if you were scared off relationships forever."

Daringly, she kissed him, brushing her lips against his. Then she opened her door and ran up the steps to her apartment. Fumbling for the keys, she had them in the lock when he caught up with her.

"Do you call that a good-night kiss?" he asked, drawing her into his arms.

His mouth searched for, then settled on hers, and Georgia joyfully stepped into his embrace and kissed him back.

Endless minutes later Dev slowly pulled away. They were both breathing hard.

"You're a dangerous woman, Georgia Brown."

"Just think about what I said," she responded, opening her door. "Good night. And thanks again for taking me."

She closed the door, realizing she'd much rather have dragged him inside with her and closed the door on the world. Listening to his footsteps move away, she wished the evening could have lasted forever.

* * *

The next morning, Georgia called Patrick.

"What's up?" her brother-in-law asked.

"Nothing yet. But Samuel Williams comes home today."

"Let me know what you discover. Rand is set to fly to the Coast next Wednesday to interview that Sam Williams. If you find out anything before then, let us know."

"I hope I can find out today," she said. Nerves were drawn tight as she thought about finally facing the man who might be her father. "How's Margot?"

"Doing fine. Want to talk to Shelby?"

"Yes."

The conversation was short, and Georgia kept listening for the sound of a car. She hadn't a clue what time to expect Dev's parents, but she wanted to be present to see them when they arrived. Would that be enough?

Hanging up the phone, Georgia moved to the window. What would Dev say if it turned out his stepfather was her real father after all?

CHAPTER SEVEN

GEORGIA deliberately delayed providing the flowers for the rooms in the main house until late Saturday morning. If she timed it right, she could still be fussing with the arrangements when Dev's parents arrived. Armed with several large vases she'd found in the garden shed and an armfull of freshly cut flowers, she entered the kitchen, explaining to Mrs. Mitton and Thelma in passing that she planned to put flowers in each of the downstairs rooms as she breezed through to the main portion of the house.

She found it fun to arrange the flowers, delighting in the visual pleasure of the various shades and hues, savoring their sweet fragrances. Georgia did her best to take her time. Stalling as long as she dared, she finally had to give up when Mrs. Mitton peeked into the dining room for the third time.

"I think all the arrangements look lovely," she said, as if puzzled by Georgia's delay.

"I want them perfect. First impressions and all," she murmured vaguely, hoping the housekeeper would attribute an anxiousness to please as the reason for her lengthy time. Where were the Williamses? Would they be home soon?

"I'm sure Mrs. Williams will love them. Will you be eating lunch with us?"

"Yes. I'm not going anywhere today." At least not before she met Sam Williams.

Mrs. Mitton didn't move until Georgia reluctantly backed away from the final arrangement.

"I guess I'm finished." She gathered the leftover blossoms and cut ends, wrapping them in the damp newspaper she'd used to keep the flowers fresh while she was arranging them.

Walking toward the gardening shed a few minutes later, Georgia looked around the yard hoping inspiration would strike. There had to be something she could do to be on hand when Dev's parents arrived without being totally obvious.

Staring at the different gardening implements, she came up with an idea. She reached for the rake. She'd pretend to work where she could watch the driveway and make sure she didn't miss anything.

It was hot. The sun beat down from a cloudless sky. Slowly she dragged the rake over and over the grass. Would Dev meet them at the airport? Unlikely with his small car. They may not even arrive until dinnertime, or later. Was she going to spend all day raking this one spot of lawn?

Fanning her face with her hand, she wondered if she could last all day. Maybe if she moved to the side of the house, she could keep the driveway in view and garner a bit of shade.

When the Williamses did arrive, Georgia almost missed them. The limo from the airport pulled quietly right up to the front door. Dashing around the side of the house when she realized what was happening, she stopped in time to see a tall man walk up the shallow steps and disappear through the front door. Mrs. Mitton was already on the stairs greeting the new arrivals, blocking him from Georgia's view.

Scarcely looking at the woman who followed him inside, Georgia felt numb. She'd glimpsed the man, and still hadn't a clue if he was her father.

"Oh, Georgia," Mrs. Mitton said as she turned to speak to the driver. "The Williamses are home."

"So I see. Can I help carry anything inside?" Georgia asked on the spur of the moment.

"The driver will take in the heavier bags. Maybe you could take this one?"

Dropping the rake, Georgia went to take the carry-on bag. Carrying it inside, she glanced around. The foyer was empty. She could hear the murmur of voices from upstairs. She was on the bottom step when Mrs. Mitton came in beside the driver.

"Oh, just put it down, Georgia. I'll get them sorted and take them upstairs later. Run along to the kitchen, Thelma has lunch ready. They would arrive just as we were ready to eat. But Thelma already has started a tray to take upstairs. Mr. Williams is going to lie down. And if I know Mrs. Williams, she's already calling Dev. I told him they'd be here this morning. But he would have to try to do some more catch-up at the office. Honestly!"

Reluctantly Georgia set the case down. With one more glance up the stairs, she headed for the kitchen. How could she be so close and yet miss them?

As soon as she finished lunch, Georgia slipped out. She was too frustrated to make conversation. Her mind was spinning with trying to come up with ways to meet Sam Williams. In retrospect, she should have held off on the flowers. She could have taken the arrangements inside once they had arrived and made sure she included a bouquet for the upstairs sitting room. Maybe she could have glimpsed the man from the open door.

Now she had no excuse for re-entering the house.

Walking back to the front yard, she picked up the rake, scanning the windows. Wouldn't Sam wish to look out over his estate? He'd been gone several weeks.

No one appeared.

Standing in the shade of the old elm, she studied the house. Which room was the master bedroom? Wasn't it the one on this corner? Dev had shown her the upstairs once, yet she felt turned around. She thought it was this room. She gazed up, wishing she could glimpse inside, just to see what the man looked like.

She thought she'd developed some patience working in medicine. But it seemed to have deserted her. She'd already been in Texas more than two weeks. She didn't want to wait any longer! There had to be a way to see the man today.

Suddenly—an idea. Five minutes later she carefully leaned the sturdy ladder from the shed against the tree. It easily reached that first solid branch. She could climb out on that limb and almost touch the house—close enough to see inside. Thanks to her escapades with Bobby Benton, she was adept at climbing trees.

"Though I never expected to play Peeping Tom," she murmured, wrestling the ladder into the precise position she wanted.

Awkwardly holding a set of pruning shears for cover in case someone spotted her, she started up the ladder. "Patrick would be proud of my resourcefulness," she mumbled as she balanced herself on the sturdy branch. If anyone caught her she'd say she was pruning.

Inching out, she was glad for her tomboy past. Climbing trees had been a lark when she was younger, but it assumed a different perspective as an adult. If she fell, she could seriously injure herself. But she wouldn't fall. And she only had a few feet more to go—

"What the hell are you doing up there?"

"What?" Georgia swayed, lost her balance and frantically reached above her to grab another limb. The shears dropped to the ground. Heart pounding, Georgia peered down through the leaves straight into Dev's face.

"You scared me to death! I could have fallen!"

Of all the rotten luck! She would have loved to see Dev at any other time. But not now!

"Why are you up there to begin with?"

Frantically she sought an excuse. "I'm cutting back some of the tree—pruning, you know."

"In August?"

Wasn't August as good a month as any other? From the disbelief in his tone, she suspected it must not the most auspicious month for pruning.

"Umm, I saw some, uh, diverticulum which is deadly for trees. I wanted to cut that out."

"Show me this diverticulum. If there is any such thing," he said stepping closer to the ladder. "Or are you up there on a spying mission?"

Color flooded her face. She couldn't say a word, only stare at him. How had he guessed?

"The problem is, you wouldn't see anything if I'm down here," he said.

"What?"

"What do you hope to see peering into my room? You saw it the other day, so why do you want to see it from this angle?"

Georgia looked at the window so tantalizingly near. The glare on the glass prevented her from seeing inside at all.

"Your room?" she squeaked. "That's your room?"

Dev laughed sardonically. "Nice touch, Georgia. As if you didn't know it's my room. Care to show me this deadly disease that threatens the tree?"

Sheer relief made her almost giddy. He thought she was trying to see into *his* room. He didn't know she wanted his father's. Inching along the limb, embarrassment swept through her. Patrick would definitely not be impressed with this escapade. But she could imagine her sisters hooting with laughter. Maybe it was something best left unrelated when she returned home.

"Ummm, actually, now that I'm up here and can see the leaves up close, I think I may have been mistaken." Slowly she made her way back to the ladder and started down.

Dev startled her when he reached up and took her around the waist, swinging her to the ground.

His smoldering eyes on her, he leaned forward. "What's really going on?"

"What do you mean?" She met his gaze, hers as impassive as she could make it. If only she didn't feel the heat staining her cheeks. "What are you doing here, anyway? With your parents' return, I thought you'd be in with them,'' she said, hoping to divert his attention.

''I came to find you so you can meet my mother.''

''Taking me home to meet Mother? Isn't this sudden?''

''She's your boss,'' he said coolly, pulling away.

She had tried to be flippant to ease some of the tension that still filled her. Now into the fray, meeting his mother—and maybe his father?

Dev walked beside Georgia wondering what she had been doing in the tree. His windows were closed. She'd seen his room, why try to peer into it? Surely that excuse about some tree disease rang false. The tree looked healthy to him.

Her sassy remark about meeting his mother brought back Elizabeth's efforts to ingratiate herself with his parents. She'd been so attentive, hanging on their every word, telling him how much she'd like to be just like his mother.

It was only later that he realized what she'd meant was be as rich as his mother. Money was the most important thing in Elizabeth's life.

Had he made a mistake in Georgia? If she thought their date Friday gave her an inside track, he'd have to set her straight. His mother was her new boss, not a prospective in-law.

Scowling, Dev lengthened his stride. Where had that thought sprung from? He had spent some time with Georgia, that's all. Nothing serious. They'd shared a couple of kisses, a few dances, a trip to the beach and one midnight swim. He certainly wasn't considering anything more involved. If they chose to spend some casual time together, it didn't automatically lead anywhere.

If and when he felt the need to get married, it would be with someone he knew wasn't in it for the money!

Rounding the corner of the house, he slowed just a bit to let Georgia take the lead. He wanted to watch her reactions when she met his mother. He could tell a lot by how a person reacted.

Ruth Williams was sitting on the patio beneath one of the large umbrellas that shaded a table. A pitcher of lemonade and several glasses were on the table. She smiled at Dev, warmth and love evident in her gaze. When she looked at Georgia, her expression became speculative, but her smile remained warm and welcoming.

"Hello, I'm Ruth Williams."

"How do you do? I'm Georgia Beau—Brown."

"Do sit down. I know you have Saturdays off, but I hope you don't mind meeting this afternoon. We'll discuss the garden plans on Monday. I just wanted to meet you today, and thank you for the lovely arrangements throughout the house. What a nice welcome home."

"I'm happy to meet you," Georgia said, sitting gingerly on the edge of the chair when Ruth indicated she should join her.

Dev pulled up a chair on the other side of his mother and sat. So far Georgia had done nothing to indicate she was trying to ingratiate herself with his mother.

Yet something felt off kilter.

Ruth poured lemonade for each of them, then settled back in her chair. "Tell me something about yourself Georgia. You seem young to be a master gardener."

She took a sip of her beverage and gave a polite smile. As she spoke, Dev's attention drifted. He liked looking at Georgia. In the shorts she wore, her long legs looked smooth and tanned. He wanted to reach out and run a fingertip along the length of her calf, feel that softness.

Thread his fingers through her silky hair and let it cascade across his palms. Cradle her head and kiss her—feeling like he'd explode with the sensations touching her always roused.

When there was a lull in the conversation, he spoke lazily, watching Georgia.

"Do you think Dad'll be up for dinner?"

"Oh, yes," Ruth replied smiling. "He really didn't want to lie down, I convinced him to do so. I know he's fully recovered, but it was such a scare that I want him to take all precautions. He'll be down for dinner. He's already asked Thelma for some of her barbecue ribs. There'll be no holding him back from those."

For a moment Dev almost asked Georgia to join them. Wouldn't that surprise his mother? She wouldn't think anything about her son dating the "hired help" like Georgia protested so often. But he wanted to wait until she knew Georgia better before springing that on her.

Since Elizabeth, if he even mentioned a woman's name, his mother got a certain hopeful look in her eye.

And a few dates and kisses did not a new daughter-in-law produce.

Not that he thought Georgia was interested in that role anyway. She was more likely to argue with him than flatter. More inclined to be difficult than compliant. And a lot more interested in hearing about his childhood than what he was doing now.

Maybe that was some of her charm. So far she had seem singularly unimpressed by his money or position.

"I've enjoyed meeting you, Georgia, but don't want to take up your weekend," Ruth said. "We'll discuss the plans for the garden on Monday. This is your day off and I'm not a slave driver."

"Seemed like it sometimes when I was a kid," Dev said, still watching Georgia. She seemed to grow more relaxed. But she still sat on the edge of her chair as if ready to dart away.

And she kept glancing at the house.

"I look forward to our working together," Ruth said graciously after frowning at her son.

Dev stood. He recognized a dismissal when he heard one.

"I'll help you carry the ladder back, if you like."

"Ladder?" Ruth asked, looking from one to the other. Georgia rose and placed her glass on the table.

"I was examining something in a tree and needed the ladder."

"Suspected diverticulum," Dev added.

Ruth frowned. "What is diverticulum? Sounds like a medical term."

"Apparently a rampant disease that can affect elms, right Georgia?" Dev answered.

"Upon closer examination, I found no trace of the disease," she said stiffly. Next time she'd have to come up with some other kind of disease. She was hitting too close to home. "Your trees look quite healthy."

Georgia walked swiftly to the ladder, frustration barely held in check. "I can manage just fine, thank you. I brought it out here, I can take it back."

"I don't mind helping you."

"I don't need your help!"

"Is the heat making you cranky?" he asked. "Or is it me?"

She stopped and glared at him. "Go visit with your mother."

Amusement swept through him. She looked like she could spit nails. He brushed the hair back from her cheek, letting his fingers linger on the soft warmth of her skin. Her cheeks were rosy and her eyes a sparkling blue.

Desire ached deep inside. Giving in to the urge, he leaned over and kissed her. His fingers threaded in her silken hair as he'd wanted, but he didn't draw her into his arms. The kiss was enough. Sweet, delicate, ardent—packing enough wallop that he suddenly craved more.

She pushed away and he let her go.

"A nice dip in the pool would cool you off," he said. It would cool him off, as well, and he could use it about now.

"No, thanks." She reached for the ladder, but Dev brushed her aside and hefted it on his shoulder. "Lead on, McDuff."

Gathering the pruning shears and rake, Georgia

stomped away. He followed, enjoying the view of her swaying hips, her long legs. Her back was ramrod straight as if to display her displeasure with him in every tantalizing inch. Instead of putting him off, it only furthered his interest. Georgia Brown was one sexy package.

The shed was stifling. Placing the ladder on its pegs, Dev quickly left, waiting while Georgia locked it shut.

"If not a swim, how about a ride?"

"Shouldn't you be with your parents? They just got back."

"They were only gone three weeks. And I'll see them at dinner. Come on, you can show me where your sister lives."

Georgia's eyes widened. "They're not home this weekend."

"So we won't stop, just drive by."

"It's too hot to be driving around with the sun beating down on us."

"So I'll put up the top, turn on the air-conditioning."

"Why have a convertible if you don't use it?"

He cupped the nape of her neck and shook her gently. "You are the most contrary woman I know. We'll have the car however you like it."

"I'd need to shower and change," she said slowly.

"Then hurry up."

She hesitated a moment, as if to argue again, then shrugged and headed for her apartment.

Dev watched her walk away, wondering what he thought he was doing spending more time with her.

The anticipation that began to build at the thought

of spending the afternoon together warned him he was getting in too deep. After today, he'd cut back on seeing Georgia. Put their relationship into perspective.

Relationship? He rubbed the back of his neck and headed for the house. Maybe he was in too deep already.

Georgia showered in record time. Slipping into a new sundress, she quickly dried and brushed her hair. Despite her failed attempts to see Sam Williams, the day felt bright and exciting. She was going to spend several hours with Dev! Maybe he'd invite her to dinner and she'd have a chance to meet his father without relying on subterfuge.

She hesitated, brush still raised as she gazed at herself in the mirror. What happened once she met the man? Would she know instantly if he were her father or not? A few judicially placed questions and she'd have an answer. Either way, she had no reason to remain in Texas after she found out the truth.

"All the more reason to make the most of this afternoon," she said, laying the brush down. This could be her final outing with Dev. Refusing to dwell on the distress the notion brought, she reached for her small purse, slipped the strap over her shoulder and headed outside.

Dev waited for her again, as he had the last time, leaning against the garage, one foot resting on the wall. He glanced up at Georgia as she ran lightly down the steps. Her heart soared when she saw him. At the same time her sense of preservation kicked in.

Don't be getting too chummy with him, she admonished herself. Futilely. She was already in over her head!

Settled in the car, top up and air conditioning on, she gazed out the window as Dev drove away from the estate, doing her best to ignore the compelling desire to gaze at him.

"Where to?" he asked

"Anywhere," she said.

"We could go to Mercer Arboretum or the Houston Arboretum. Both have exhibits of native Texas plants. Is that something you'd like?"

"Would you?"

He shrugged. "Plants aren't my life, but I thought you might enjoy seeing the local indigenous varieties. Or we could drive through Heights and see samples of Victorian gardens. Or try something totally different and head for the Space Center."

She laughed softly. "You sound like a tour guide."

"At your service, ma'am."

"If it weren't so hot, I'd say let's head for one of the arboretums."

"There'll be plenty of shade."

Touched he chose a spot for her benefit, Georgia resolved to enjoy herself. She wasn't highly interested in plants, but he didn't know that. And she did enjoy looking at gardens. Today it was his company she craved more than anything. She would take what he offered, greedily hoarding every memory.

And maybe learn a bit more about Dev Tolliver.

"Where did you go to school?" she asked.

"High school here in Houston, college at the University in Austin." He turned on the station playing soft jazz.

"Did you ever work on the oil rigs like your father?"

"A couple of summers, nothing like he did. He said the experience was good for the business, but beyond that, it didn't contribute to working in an office."

"Did you like it?"

"Yeah, it was hot and hard work, but challenging."

"Yet you find working at the main office challenging, too, don't you?"

"In a different way. Do you find your work challenging?"

Nursing?

"Yes. I'm still so new at it, I know I don't have all the knowledge or experience I need. But I do the best I can, and still study."

He glanced at her, frowning slightly. "With several years experience, I'd think you'd feel more confident."

The cover story! "Well, I still think there's lots I don't know."

"There are a lot of men who work as landscape architects, I'm surprised you haven't found one to suit you."

"What does that mean?"

"I'm still curious why you aren't married."

"Maybe I think I'm better off on my own. What's your excuse?"

"I told you—"

"No, Dev, I mean what really happened? Did she cheat on you? Or throw you over for someone else? Whatever it was, you are sure anti-marriage now."

"Not so. My folks have a great marriage. Just as a marriage is supposed to be, open, loving, committed. They have a lot in common, share interests, friends.''

''And you didn't have that with your fiancée?''

He turned into the parking lot of the arboretum, pulling into a shady spot and killing the engine. Turning slightly he looked at Georgia.

''Elizabeth was perfection. She liked everything I liked, wanted to do everything I wanted to do. The perfect corporate wife—good at working a room at a party, always supportive.''

''But?''

''But she was in it for the money. For what my money would buy her. She wanted a glamorous life-style, and picked me as the man most likely to give it to her. And she worked hard at being the perfect woman for me. Only—there was no emotion, no feelings, and certainly no commitment!''

''Oh.''

''Oh? Is that all you have to say? Would you treat a man like that, Georgia? Would you lead him on with an agenda of your own? Pretend he is all you want, when in reality it's what he can provide that you want?''

''Not all women are like that.''

''That's true. But enough are.''

''So you'll wait for a woman who can buy and sell your father before becoming involved.''

''Right.''

''What if she suspects you are after her money?''

He studied her for a moment. ''Interesting thought, isn't it? Come on.''

Georgia ached for the younger Dev, who had loved Elizabeth enough to ask her to marry him before discovering she didn't love him. He was a proud man, taking pride in his accomplishments, in his own innate integrity. It must have hurt a lot.

She wanted to gather him close and soothe away that old hurt.

And he'd probably laugh until the middle of next week if she tried.

Taking his hand, she squeezed it a bit. It was the most she could offer.

Dev laced his fingers through hers, but said nothing as they walked toward the entrance.

The afternoon was perfect, Georgia realized a little while later. They wandered alone on one of the paths, shaded by the old trees. The planting beds were full of colorful flowers that she hadn't a clue what to call. So far Dev had not asked her to identify any plants. She hoped her luck held.

He seemed relaxed, and she enjoyed the small talk they exchanged. She'd say more, but she was still wary of his remembering the voice of the woman on the phone. It seemed like another lifetime when she had first called him. Yet it was just over two weeks.

Amazing. Now she couldn't imagine not knowing Dev.

Not loving him.

Georgia froze. Dev took two steps, his arm outstretched with hers, before he realized she'd stopped.

"What's wrong?"

She blinked and looked at him. Her heart beat a furious tempo. She couldn't have fallen in love that fast. And not with Dev Tolliver. Averting her eyes, she tried to summon a smile.

"Nothing's wrong, I just want to study this flower

for a minute.'' But her eyes couldn't focus on the blue blossom.

She tried to slow her rapid pulse. Tried to think rationally.

But the fact wouldn't go away. She was in love with Dev Tolliver.

Falling in love with him was probably the dumbest mistake she'd ever made.

CHAPTER EIGHT

SHE wanted to go home. To escape the emotions that threatened to overwhelm her. To gain some solitude in order to think through her amazing discovery. How could she have let herself fall in love? Dev had made it abundantly clear he had no interest in marriage—and especially not with her.

And the sudden thought of all the years ahead that wouldn't hold Dev in her life dismayed her.

"I need to get back," she said stiffly.

"Are you all right?"

"I think the heat is getting to me." As an excuse it was feeble, but it would have to do. She needed some space—and time to think.

Not that thinking would change anything. There was no future with Dev. She knew the futility of wishful thinking. Hadn't she been present when a patient wouldn't respond to treatment? Hadn't she railed against fate more than once—to discover it never changed things?

The ride home seemed interminable. Georgia silently urged Dev to drive faster. His presence fed her dismay. She yearned to be more than a casual date—to mean something to him, become important in his life.

Dev looked over at her several times, as if to check that she was still there. The air-conditioning in the car cooled her, but she refused to meet his gaze.

"You can use the pool tonight if you like. My parents usually go to bed around eleven, so a midnight swim wouldn't be detected."

"Thanks."

Go swimming again? Remember the night they'd shared the pool? She didn't think that was something she wanted to do. She had enough memories to make her ache with longing, no sense deliberately adding to her turmoil.

Was there another way?

Of course it would be hard to show up one day three years younger and with a nursing degree.

Who was she fooling? He had no interest in her beyond a casual date here and there. If there were strong feelings on both sides, they could work things out. But he'd never given a hint he was growing to care for her. To him, she was a novelty. When he looked for a wife, it would be in the echelons of the rich and famous.

Could she win a lottery?

Wait a minute! Did she truly want a man who thought money was so important he wouldn't even look at a woman unless she matched his net worth?

In a heartbeat—if it was Dev, she admitted.

He pulled into the spot where he normally parked and stopped the engine.

"Thank you. I had a nice time."

"Ever the proper response," he murmured, brushing the back of his fingers along her cheek. "Are you going to be all right?"

"I'll be fine." She opened the door and almost ran to the stairs. But being alone didn't help, all her thoughts centered on Dev.

Eating a sandwich later for dinner, Georgia restlessly roamed around the tiny apartment, feeling alone
and abandoned. She had tried calling her sisters, but
neither was at home. Not that they could do much,
but she longed to hear their familiar voices, listen to
Margot's advice, or Shelby's calm suggestions.

She needed to get this over with. She felt stretched
tight as a drum. Maybe tonight. She'd calmly walk
up to Sam Williams and—

Her mind went blank.

No matter what, she couldn't imagine what she'd
say. She'd just have to hope something came to mind
when she was on the spot.

Walking out into the evening heat, she wandered
around the yard, wishing she knew more about taking
care of the plants. She looked up when she neared
the patio. The aroma of barbecue wafted on the air.
Her mouth watered. A sandwich didn't compare with
a Texas barbecue.

Screened from the patio by the high hedge that ran
along one side, she drew close without anyone seeing
her.

Yet she could see them through the leaves. Dev
and his parents sat around one of the large tables. Sam
had his back to her. She could see him gesturing. A
minute later Ruth and Dev burst out laughing.

Georgia watched for a long time. She and her sisters had rarely enjoyed eating outside. It was not
something their grandmother had approved of. And
there had been no laughing or such obvious enjoy-
ment when they'd dined at Beaufort Hall—everything
had been much too formal.

Georgia found her gaze resting on Dev. He looked

relaxed, amused, happy. Obviously his family had a close bond.

Except with her sisters, she had never felt such a tie. Which made her feel sad and envious—and even more lonely.

Turning away, she knew she wouldn't approach Sam Williams tonight. She would not be the one to disrupt such a happy setting. There was always tomorrow.

Georgia didn't feel like sleep. She tried to read the gardening book, but threw it aside after a few pages.

Heading for the bedroom, she began to pack her things. There wasn't much, only the few shorts and sundresses she'd bought since she'd been in Texas. Of course the dress she'd worn to the party couldn't be crushed in a suitcase. Touching it lightly, she smiled wistfully. Another memory to tuck away.

The knock on the door startled her. Knowing instinctively who it was before she opened it, she couldn't control the delight that filled her.

"Hi." He leaned against the jamb, looking down at her with those sexy silvery-gray eyes.

"Hi." Original. Why couldn't she be different, fascinating. Beguiling? Make him so crazy for her he'd overlook everything?

"Want to go swimming?"

No, no, no. The last thing she needed was to put herself anywhere near a half-naked man who already drove her crazy.

"Sure. I'll meet you there in a few minutes. I need to change." Was that voice hers? What happened to no?

"I'll wait." Pushing her gently, he backed her into the apartment and closed the door behind him.

"Are your parents asleep?" A quick glance at the clock showed it was not that late.

"In bed in any event. My mother likes to read before falling asleep and I noticed the light is on in their room."

"Oh. I'll just be a minute."

Slipping into the silken water a few moments later, Georgia threw caution to the wind. One more night couldn't hurt. She couldn't fall any more in love. And to spend a precious few hours with Dev seemed only fair when she would soon be back in New Orleans—all alone.

They swam, then held on to the side of the pool and talked softly. Reluctant to leave the water, almost floating, Georgia let her legs entangle with Dev's. Darkness cloaked them, the stars sparkling in the distance the only witness. The bedroom light had been extinguished long ago.

When he reached for her, Georgia moved into his arms with no hesitation. Encircling his neck, she kissed him with abandon, letting her love consume them both.

Dev let go of the side to hold her and they sank beneath the water.

Laughing and splashing, they surfaced.

"That's one way to cool off," she said, grabbing for the side.

"Let's move to the shallow end," he said, kicking away and swimming to the other end of the pool on his back, his gaze never leaving hers.

Georgia followed slowly. She was playing with

wildfire, but she didn't care. This could be her last night in Texas. Why not spend it with the man she loved?

Dev was waiting when she swam to him, pulling her quickly into his arms to kiss her. His lips were cool, but quickly warmed. His tongue swept inside her mouth to tantalize and excite. Giving in to the ardor that arose, Georgia traced the muscles in his shoulders, across his chest. Reveling in the sensations that filled her, she wished the moment could last a lifetime.

"I want you, Georgia," Dev said, kissing a trail across her wet cheek. "Let's become lovers."

Her heart stopped, skipped a beat then raced.

Pulling back, she tried to see him, but he was silhouetted against the stars, she could not see into his eyes, judge his expression.

"Lovers?" she repeated, stunned.

"You're attracted to me, I'm attracted to you. There's something explosive between us, Georgia. Let me come back to your apartment and make love to you."

For one glorious moment, Georgia almost said yes. Dev wanted her! He wanted them to become lovers!

But reality crashed down. Dev had not mentioned *love*.

"You want to become lovers, does that mean fall in love, the whole bit?" she asked.

He shook his head, cradling her head in his palms. "I want you, Georgia. More and more every time I see you. We're both single adults, unattached, uncommitted. Why not share this attraction? You can't deny you feel it, too."

"Attraction? Maybe what I feel is love," she said slowly, wishing she could see his expression, gauge how her words impacted him.

Dev's harsh laughter sounded loud in the quiet night. "Not you, too? I thought you were different. So now it's *love*?"

Georgia disengaged herself from his hold and moved through the water to the steps. Climbing from the pool, she refused to give in to the incredible hurt his laughter and scornful words generated.

Picking up her towel, she wrapped it around sarong style and wrung the water from her hair. Amazed she was even functioning with the blossoming pain in her heart, she watched him warily as he followed her from the pool.

"So the answer is no?" Dev asked, keeping his distance.

"You know what, Dev? You're a very special person. And you deserve happiness. I hope you find it. But scoffing at the genuine feelings of others is not real conducive to that end. Is it so unbelievable that someone could fall in love with you? I think you are a wonderful man. I wish—"

She bit her lip and shook her head. "I wish things had been different, that's all. Good night."

Hurrying across the lawn, Georgia felt numb. He wanted to become lovers, but not be in love. How could she give herself to someone who refused to give a part of himself back?

Had she misjudged him? Was he not worthy of her love? Had she only loved an illusion?

The next morning Georgia finished breakfast before she saw Dev and Ruth walking toward the garage. A few minutes later they drove away. From the clothes they wore, and the time, she suspected they were going to church.

But not Sam.

This would be the perfect time to find Samuel Williams—alone.

Without further thought, Georgia headed down the stairs. Stopping in the shed to get some clippers, she cut an armful of flowers, keeping her eye on the time. She entered the house through the kitchen.

Thelma was absent. Mrs. Mitton sat reading the Sunday paper as she sipped from a cup of coffee.

"Good morning," she said, looking up at Georgia and the flowers. "More flowers? I thought you filled every room."

"Just one more. Mrs. Williams said she liked filling the house with them." Hoping she looked more confident than she felt, she breezed through and into the main house. Pausing to listen carefully, she heard nothing. Taking a deep breath, she headed for the steps. She'd knock before entering the sitting room. And just maybe the connecting door would be open.

A noise from the office stopped her. Turning, she walked to the open door and peered inside.

An older man sat behind the desk, perusing some papers. He had a touch of silver at his temples and the weathered skin of someone who spent a lot of time out of doors. He looked a bit thin, but Georgia attributed that to his recent illness. His clothes weren't that loose, attesting to the fact he was probably in good physical condition normally.

"Hello," she said, her heart in her throat.

He raised his head, hazel eyes looking quizzically at her. Georgia tried to absorb every detail so she could tell Margot and Shelby if he was the one.

"Hello, you must be Georgia Brown, our new gardener. My wife said she met you yesterday. I'm Samuel Williams." He rose and smiled easily, holding out his hand.

Georgia nodded, stepping inside and shaking his hand quickly.

"I thought you might like to have some flowers in here." She felt tongue-tied, shy, awkward. How did one go about asking a stranger if he were her father?

"That was thoughtful. I don't often have flowers in here."

Georgia looked around. She had forgotten a vase.

"I'll be right back, I need a vase."

Fleeing to the kitchen, she tried to get control of her emotions. If the man was not her father, he'd think her a blithering idiot. And if he were, she wanted him to be interested enough to talk to her, not suspect she needed a keeper.

Taking a vase back into the office a few moments later, Georgia set it on a bookcase and began to place flowers into it.

Sam had begun to read again. Should she talk? Or remain silent? She glanced at him, trying to see something that would tell her he was the one.

He looked up, leaned back in his chair.

"I understand you've been seeing Dev."

She blinked. That was the last thing she'd expected him to say.

"I'm not sure *seeing him* is the right phrase. We've spent a little time together. He was staying here, I

have the garage apartment.'' She shrugged, not wanting to even think about Dev at this moment.

Samuel motioned Georgia to sit down. She perched
on the edge of one of the comfortable wing-back
chairs near the window and watched him warily. Now
what?

''Mrs. Mitton seems to feel differently. She spoke
about it to Ruth.''

''Oh.'' Georgia looked at her hands trying to figure
how to answer while wondering what exactly Mrs.
Mitton had said.

''You're the first woman who's taken Dev's eye in
a long time.''

''Since Elizabeth, you mean?'' she asked, looking
at him.

''So he told you about Elizabeth?''

Georgia nodded. ''I think it really hit him hard.''

''Nonsense, she was a blatant little gold digger
looking for a free ride. He caught on to her before
they tied the knot.''

''Maybe not fast enough,'' she murmured, thinking
of his philosophy of marriage. A man who hadn't
been burned badly would never consider he had to
match bank accounts before he could trust his feelings.

''Have we met before?'' Sam asked. He looked at
her thoughtfully.

''I don't think so. I'm from New Orleans. Have
you been there recently?''

He shook his head, still staring at her. ''Not for
several years. But there's something...''

''Have you lived in Texas your entire life?'' she

asked. She remembered what Dev had said, but would Sam tell her something different?

"Most of it. Came from Montana originally. Winters up there are too damn cold for me. I like the southern states."

"States? Have you lived in more than one?"

Was it her imagination, or had he grown more guarded? "A few. What brings you to Texas?"

You, Georgia wanted to say, but her courage failed her. "Family."

She tried to find a resemblance between this man and her sisters or herself. Maybe the hair color was close to Margot's. Maybe the jaw reminded her of Shelby's.

Or maybe she was just indulging in wishful thinking. She seemed to be doing it a lot lately.

"Here you are, Mr. Williams." Mrs. Mitton entered carrying a silver tray with coffee and sweet rolls. "Got to build back your strength and weight," she said, placing the tray on his desk.

"I can bring a cup for Georgia if you like," she said, glancing at Georgia.

"Do, we're chatting about things. I'm hoping she'll bring up my son soon," he said with a twinkle in his eye.

The housekeeper laughed. "You just wait until you see them together, then you'll know." She was still chuckling when she left the room.

"I don't need to stay," Georgia said, jumping up. "I'll just finish the flowers and leave you to your coffee."

"Now don't run off. Ruth and Dev have gone to church and I'm alone in the house."

"Except for Mrs. Mitton and Thelma," Georgia said, poking another stem into the vase.

"But I've known them for years. It's you I'm curious about. What have you and Dev been up to?"

"An afternoon at the beach and one party thrown by one of your vendors, hardly anything important."

"The Titan annual event? Isn't that interesting?"

She started to tell him interesting didn't describe things, that she had fallen in love with his stepson. But it was not his business. If Dev didn't believe her, why would anyone else?

Stuffing the last of the flowers into the vase, ignoring their ragged appearance, Georgia gathered the cut ends and dumped them in the small trash can standing beside the desk.

Subtlety was obviously not her forte. She didn't know how to get the information she wanted without coming right out and asking.

"Did you ever live—"

Mrs. Mitton bustled in, carrying a cup of coffee. "I put cream in it like you drink it, Georgia."

The phone rang.

Georgia closed her mouth, reached for the cup and gave Mrs. Mitton a polite smile. "Thank you."

She tried to ignore Sam's side of the conversation as she sipped her coffee. When he hung up, she'd ask him if he had ever lived in Mississippi. If he said no, she'd let it go. Or would he say that anyway? Did he still believe there was a murder charge? Wouldn't he have changed his name and tried to keep a low profile if that was the case? Yet if he knew the real murderer had been apprehended, why had he stayed away?

"That was my wife. She's joined friends for lunch.

I'll need to tell Thelma,'' he said as he hung up the phone. ''Unless you'd care to join us? Dev will be home in a few minutes. We eat at one.''

''You'd ask the gardener to Sunday dinner?'' she exclaimed before she could stop herself. Her grandmother never sat down a day in her life with the hired help. Even Caroline, who had worked for her for years.

''Not normally, but I think I'm inviting someone Dev is interested in.''

I want you, Georgia, Dev's words echoed in her mind. Was that interest?

''What do you say?'' Sam asked.

''About what?'' Dev stood in the doorway, his gaze fixed on Georgia.

''Nothing.'' She jumped up and placed her cup and saucer on the edge of the desk, starting toward the door, anxious to escape. The last thing she planned to do was confront Sam in front of an audience. Throwing him a brief glance, she tried to smile. ''Thanks anyway.''

Dev didn't move. Georgia couldn't get through the door with him blocking it.

''Excuse me.''

''What are you doing here?'' he asked suspiciously.

''I brought in some more flowers. Would you please move?''

He looked across the room at the vase with the haphazardly placed flowers. ''Not as neat an arrangement as in the other rooms,'' he commented.

''So fix it yourself,'' she said, standing close

enough to feel the heat of his body. "Would you move?" she said through her teeth.

The air almost shimmered between them. Georgia longed to throw herself into his arms and have him hold her as if he'd never let her go. Did his stepfather suspect? How could anyone not pick up on the attraction they shared? It seemed to hum between them.

Dev had to pick up on it, too. He looked at her for a long moment, then stepped aside. When Georgia hurried from the room, he kept pace with her, catching her arm near the bottom of the stairs and swinging her around to face him.

"I haven't changed my mind," he said, kissing her before she could say a word.

"Nor have I," she whispered when he raised his head. Involuntarily she brushed her fingertips against his lips and then turned to leave.

"Have dinner with me. We can talk," he said stiffly.

She glanced over her shoulder. He stood ramrod straight at the foot of the stairs, his expression schooled to reveal nothing.

I want you, Georgia. He might as well have shouted it, she heard it echo so clearly in her mind.

"I think conversation would be futile."

"Have dinner with me," he practically ordered.

"And if I don't?"

A glimmer of amusement shone in his eyes. "I might have known it wouldn't be easy. Do you ever do anything the easy way?"

Warily she watched him. She was not answering that comment.

"I'll pick you up at seven," he said.

Without waiting for a response, he turned and went back to the den. A moment later she heard the murmur of the men's voices. Were they talking about her?

Sunday afternoon had seemed endless, Georgia thought as she followed Dev into the elevator of his apartment building shortly after seven. The car whisked them quickly to the twentieth floor. The hall was spacious, quiet, and empty. When he unlocked his door, he stood aside to allow her to enter.

Compared to her tiny apartment in Metairie, his place was palatial. The living room was comprised of a wall of windows giving a sweeping view of Houston and the flat landscape that extended as far as she could see. To the left she saw a small dining area and beyond that a kitchen.

"This is great," she said, examining everything, from the landscapes that adorned the walls, to the thick chocolate-brown carpeting underfoot. The sofa and chair were heavy Spanish style, solid and comfortable. The coffee table in front of the sofa showed signs of wear.

A large-screen television sat in the corner, beside a stereo setup that looked complicated. Business journals, paperback books and a few hardcover books were evident.

Georgia turned around and smiled at him, hoping he couldn't tell how nervous she felt. "This looks like you. Solid and strong."

"That makes me sound like a plow horse."

"Would you rather be thought dashing and reckless?"

"Dashing's not bad. And I definitely feel reckless tonight, don't you?"

"A bit." Flustered by the look in his eye, she glanced toward the kitchen. "I smell something wonderful. What's for dinner?"

"Shish kebab, wild rice and a salad. Chocolate mousse for dessert."

She looked at him, her eyes widening. "Wow, I didn't know you could cook. That sounds terrific!"

He inclined his head once.

Something about it clued her in.

"Did you cook it?" she asked suspiciously.

"It's in my kitchen, why wouldn't I cook it?"

"You didn't prepare it, did you?" she guessed.

"Doesn't warming it up count as cooking?"

Georgia laughed. "Thelma?"

"Trust me, Georgia, you wouldn't want to try my cooking. I'm pretty good at boiling an egg, but somehow miss the nuances of cooking more than one thing and having everything ready at the same time."

Her smile faded and she studied him. "I do trust you, Dev. The thing is I think you need to trust yourself."

He walked into the kitchen. Georgia followed, standing against the island counter watching as he checked the oven.

"You said we would talk," she reminded him.

"We will, but let's eat first."

Like the lull before the storm, Georgia thought.

"Okay. What can I do to help?"

For the next few minutes they worked together companionably in the small kitchen. If he brushed against her more frequently than was strictly necessary, she didn't mind. Each touch brought a new shiver of awareness and growing anticipation.

If she bumped into him a couple of times, it was accidental, despite how much she liked his hands coming up to steady her. For a little while she let herself imagine them preparing dinner together every night. They wouldn't have to rely on Thelma's cooking, Georgia could cook.

They'd eat, talk over their day, then retire to the bedroom and close the world behind them.

It was a lovely daydream, she thought as he seated her at the table. Candles had been lit, the places set beside each other. When he dimmed the overhead light, Georgia realized how romantic the man could be. Did he have a clue? It was delightful for a woman to feel so cherished.

Yet always in the back of her mind was the looming talk. Would they clear the air, or only confuse things even more?

CHAPTER NINE

DEV ate slowly, watching Georgia. She seemed on edge, but he couldn't fault that. He'd caused it with his blatant invitation last night. Even now, he wasn't certain why she'd refused. She was attracted to him. He knew that from her flirtatious looks, the touches in the kitchen, the way she blushed sometimes when he looked at her.

And all of it made him want her even more.

But he wasn't falling for the love fallacy. Why did women want to hear some undying commitment before giving in to their own needs? He wanted her, she wanted him, it was simple. Neither had anyone it would hurt.

Unless she was holding out for something more.

"This is delicious," Georgia said.

"I'll let Thelma know you like it." He smiled. She'd seen right through his deception. Not that he truly wanted her to believe he could cook. Honesty was important in any relationship.

Damn, there was that word again.

"Why the frown?" she asked. "Don't you like it?"

"Just a disquieting thought." When she resumed eating he watched her. It felt right to be eating with her. To work in the kitchen together.

But feeling right tonight and a long-term commitment were two vastly different things.

As far as he knew, she didn't have any money. Was she hoping to change that by luring him into some kind of relationship? Were all women like Elizabeth? Or was Georgia different?

Dev suggested they take their coffee and brandy into the living room after stacking the dishes in the sink when they'd finished eating. Sinking down on the comfortable sofa, Georgia half turned toward him, tucking her feet up on the cushions.

"So let's have it," she said. "We've eaten and if I have to end up walking home, I don't want it to be too late."

He sat beside her, close enough to touch her knees, her breasts almost brushing against his arm. She wanted to talk and he wanted to kiss her, hold her, make love to her. Be surrounded by Georgia until he forgot the rest of the world and could only see her.

"You're not going to be walking home. I'll take you. The question is when."

"When?"

"Tonight—or tomorrow morning?"

He watched the color rise in her cheeks. Touching her lightly with his fingertips, he expected to be scorched, but she was only warm.

She held his gaze. Dev knew enough about poker to know when to hold. He'd made his interest clear. The next move was up to her. Though if he didn't know better, he'd almost suspect she was shy. But no woman reached her age without having some involvement with men. No doubt this contrary woman would surprise him with her response.

"Tonight, then," she said almost sadly.

Dev sighed and leaned his head back against the cushions, closing his eyes. "Damn," he said softly.

She giggled.

Opening his eyes, he rolled his head to the right to glare at her. "It's not funny."

"I'm nervous. I've never had someone want me so much."

"What do you mean never? Are the men in New York blind?"

She smiled broadly, catching her lower lip between her teeth. That almost sent Dev through the roof. He'd like to tug gently on that full lower lip with his own teeth, cover her mouth with his and taste the sweet delight he'd found before.

"You're terrific for a woman's ego," she said, lightly tracing a pattern on his cheek with a fingertip.

Dev reached up and clasped her hand, bringing it down and lacing his fingers through hers. Her palm was warm, her hand small in his, yet capable. She was nothing like Elizabeth. Dare he risk more than a casual involvement?

"But I can't," she said, her eyes gravely serious. "We both have things in the way—you with your hang-up about people liking you only because of the money. And me—well, I have something to tell you, but you're going to be furious. Will this attraction we feel be strong enough to last?"

Dev's heart sank. She was married.

"Tell me, and see."

"Not tonight. This is just for us. We can spend a few hours together, then you can take me home and come back here in plenty of time to get a good night's sleep for work tomorrow."

He shook his head. "I don't need a lot of sleep. Stay."

He could see the hesitation, almost feel the warring factions within her. Part of her wanted to, he was sure of that. Maybe she was playing hard to get.

She tugged her hand, but he refused to release her. He wanted the close contact, wanted to know how she felt as her expression changed. Wanted to make her desire him as much as he desired her.

"If you're married, just go ahead and say it!" he ordered.

"Married? Me? No, I'm not married. I just finished my training. I sure didn't have time to get married."

"Training? To be a gardener?" He didn't examine the sense of relief her words brought. She was single, just as he was.

Pulling gently, he tumbled her off balance and against his chest. His arms pulled her close and his mouth found hers with unerring instinct. Despite her reluctance to become involved, her kiss was hot and exciting. She held nothing back and he threaded his fingers through her hair, holding her just where he wanted while he traced her lips then slipped between them with his tongue. She was sweet as natural honey, warm as the Texas sun.

And his.

He just had to convince her of that fact.

Slowly Georgia shook her head and pulled back.

"Dev, we'd better stop. I'm trying to do what I think is right, but you don't make it easy for me to even remember my own name." She pushed away and stood up, trying to straighten her dress, avoiding his gaze.

He debated arguing with her. But tonight wasn't the only night they'd have together. Her kiss had been as passionate as anything he'd ever experienced. Maybe he could play her waiting game.

But not patiently.

Rising, he towered over her, frustration filling him. "How long will this go on?"

"What?" she asked, stepping back, bumping the coffee table. Her purse fell on the far side, its contents spilling across the rug.

"Playing hot and cold. You're not indifferent. You may say one thing, but your lips don't lie when we kiss. You want me, too."

"Yes, you're right. But for different reasons."

Her words from the night before echoed in his mind. *Maybe what I feel is love.*

"I don't love you. I've never pretended that I do," Dev said.

"I know. I never asked you to say it."

"But you want me to," he pushed, his frustration growing.

She shrugged, trying to act indifferent, but he could see the hurt in her eyes. "You've done nothing to lead me on. Good heavens, you practically wear a sign saying you distrust all women. If I fell in love, that's my business. But I do have to protect myself any way I can, and making love with you would make it twice as hard to walk away afterward."

The thought of her walking away almost forced a denial from him. He didn't want her leaving. He wanted to be able to see her every day, watch her eyes light up when he entered a room, track the color as it flushed her cheeks when he teased her. Wanted to share her passion in the night, and her sunny disposition each morning.

Was he falling in love with Georgia Brown despite all his efforts to the contrary?

"I'd better go," she said. Looking around, she spotted her purse and contents.

Dev rounded the table and began to gather things up and hand them to her. Georgia stuffed them into her purse.

When he picked up her wallet, she reached out to snatch it from his hand. It fell open—her Louisiana driver's license clearly displayed.

"Give me that," she said, reaching for it again.

Dev swung around, moving it out of her reach as he captured her hand in his. He read the license again.

Beaufort? Where had he heard that name before?

Swinging back he stared at her.

"Who are you?" he asked.

Georgia cleared her throat, her expression similar to a deer caught in headlights, terrified, yet mesmerized, unable to move.

His eyes fixed on hers, he saw her take a deep breath, slowly exhale.

"I'm Georgia Beaufort. My sisters and I think Sam Williams may be our father."

"Well, he isn't. What scam are you trying to run?"

"Let me explain, Dev," she said in her normal Southern drawl. There was no use for pretense any longer. She watched his eyes widen in disbelief. "Just listen for a minute! I told you I have two sisters, older sisters. Our mother died just after I was born. I've seen pictures of her, but don't remember a thing about her. And there were no pictures of our father. Grandmother destroyed all of them.''

"You were an orphan and your grandmother raised all three girls, I remember. But what does that have to do with your being here, and claiming my father is yours?"

"Actually, that's only part right. I'm not an orphan. I think I have a father living. My brother-in-law Patrick is a private investigator and he narrowed down the list to three men. The one in New Jersey isn't the right man. Now it's down to two. Your step-father might be the one."

"I thought you said your father had died."

"I said, he'd gone before my mother. I let you think I meant he died, but what I meant was literally that—he'd gone before my mother died. Gone, left, disappeared. All my life I thought he'd abandoned us before I was even born. But we found out last spring that he had not left of his own volition. He had been forced to leave or face a murder charge."

"Your father committed a *murder*?"

She shook her head. "Of course not. I should have said face a *bogus* murder charge. It's long and in-volved and complicated and I don't want to go into it all right now. But the fact is he was forced to leave because of my grandmother's interference. She wanted her only daughter to marry into an old Mississippi family with a heritage and lots of money.''

"Mississippi?"

"Margot found out most of the story when she and Rand cleared up our grandmother's estate. Shelby married Patrick so he'd help us locate our father. And I'm here because we think we have.''

Dev glared at her. His grip tightened convulsively on her hand.

"Suddenly it all makes sense. The endless questions. The fascination with my upbringing. You're that woman who phoned me at the office and tried to convince me you're my stepfather's daughter.''

He wanted to throw something. Howl at the moon! Damnation! He had begun to care for Georgia Brown.

"Your name isn't Georgia Brown. So let me guess, you're not a gardener either.''

She shook her head. "A nurse.''

"How dare you try to worm your way into our home, our lives, to set yourself up as a long-lost daughter! What happened? Did you see that as a long shot once you heard he was doing better? Decide getting involved with me offered a better chance? Easier to have me make a play for you than convince my father he had a daughter?''

"Actually, three daughters," Georgia said, trying to pry his hand from hers. "Let me go, Dev.''

"Get your purse, we're leaving. You can pack your bags tonight and hit the road. The deception didn't work. You're lucky I don't call the police. I may yet.''

She finally pulled her hand free.

"I didn't expect to fall in love with you. I wouldn't do anything until you knew, Dev. Please listen to me.''

He shook his head. "The time for talking is over. We'll take a full inventory of everything in the house. If anything is missing you'll be our first suspect.''

Georgia stood, her chin raised, her eyes glaring right back. "Nothing is missing, and I'm not leaving until I find out for sure if this Samuel Williams is my father."

"*This* Samuel Williams? How many are there?"

"If you'd been listening you would have heard me a minute ago. Patrick narrowed the list to three. We didn't have a lot to go on. Apparently they all worked for Sinjin Oil out of New Orleans at one time. The company records were burned, but Patrick thought one of the three men was the right one. He checked out the one in New Jersey, Rand is checking on the one in California, I drew Texas."

"Nice try, lady, but I've already answered your questions. My dad is not the man you're looking for. Try your scam somewhere else."

"Ask him," she said. "Just ask him. Or let me."

"No way, get your things, we're leaving." He handed her the wallet.

"Dev, this doesn't finish it. One way or another, sooner or later, Patrick or Rand or I will speak with your father. You can be present, or not, your choice. But I deserve to know for sure. My sisters deserve to know. And maybe even our father would think he deserves to know. We don't understand why he stayed away, but whatever the reason, we *deserve* to know."

"I'll call your bluff," Dev said, reaching out to pick up a phone. He quickly dialed.

"Hi, Mom, is Dad around? No, just wanted to check something with him." He held Georgia's gaze, covering the mouthpiece while he waited. "What was your mother's name?"

"Ask him if he knew Amanda Beaufort from Natchez, Mississippi."

"Hi, Dad. I've got a woman here who claims to be your long-lost daughter. She says to ask you if you ever knew an Amanda Beaufort from Natchez, Mississippi."

Dev felt his world tilt when his father replied.

"She was my first wife. We had two daughters. I haven't seen them in more than twenty years. Which one is looking for me? Bring her by the house, son."

"We'll be right there," Dev said slowly. He hung up, his eyes still locked with Georgia's. Her gaze became compassionate. She reached out as if to touch him, then dropped her hand. Tears began to fill her eyes.

"He's my father, isn't he?" she asked, biting her lower lip when it began to tremble. "My whole life I've missed having a daddy. Now I've found him, haven't I?"

"So it appears."

He'd been wrong, she *was* exactly like Elizabeth. Once again, he had not been what a woman had wanted—only the means to an end.

When Dev pulled into the driveway, he drove straight to the front door, not stopping by the garage. Every light on the ground floor seemed to be on. The outside lights as well. He stopped the car at the foot of the steps.

"So the prodigal returns," he said scathingly.

Georgia looked at him. "Not exactly. But I do want to talk to him. I'm not taking away your father, Dev. I'm only claiming mine."

"We'll see exactly what you're after, won't we?"

He opened his door and headed for the house. Georgia watched him pass the car and recognized his deliberate lack of manners as the slap he no doubt intended. Had she gained a father and lost a love?

No, she thought pragmatically as she opened her door and stepped out, she'd never had the love.

Before Dev could open the front door it swung wide, Ruth and Samuel standing in the light.

Georgia stopped dead, scared. She wished her sisters were with her.

"Dad, Mom, meet Georgia Beaufort. Apparently a long-lost daughter."

Samuel glanced at Dev, hearing the bitterness in his tone. Then he looked at Georgia.

"I don't have a daughter named Georgia."

"Actually, you do," she said, climbing the shallow steps. "I was born seven months after you were driven away by Harriet Beaufort. Margot and Shelby are my older sisters. Amanda Beaufort was my mother. How do you do?" She held out her hand, hoping no one noticed how it shook.

Samuel hesitated only a second before enfolding her into his arms. She felt Ruth hug them both.

"Oh, Samuel, one of your daughters! I'm so happy for you, my love," she said softly.

Samuel eased Georgia back until he held her shoulders. Gazing into her eyes, he nodded. "I should have known instantly when we talked earlier. You have a look of your mother."

"That's why I seemed familiar?"

"Your eyes are just like Amanda's."

"As are Margot's and Shelby's. We don't look alike except for the Beaufort eyes."

"I can't believe I never heard of you. Amanda should have told me she was pregnant with you. She owed me that much at least."

"Maybe we should go sit down, darling. I'm sure we all want to hear everything. And Georgia probably has questions as well," Ruth said, closing the door, glancing at her son.

"I have plenty of questions myself," Dev said, his arms folded, his expression once again impassive. "And not just for Georgia."

He was blazing angry, she knew. But she had more than she could deal with at the moment with her own emotions. Her *father* had his arm around her shoulders. Her *father* was walking with her into his living room.

Samuel and Ruth exchanged a look. "I'm sure you do, son. It could be a long evening. Ask Thelma to fix us a pot of coffee and bring something to eat," Samuel said as he passed with Georgia in the circle of his arm.

Ten minutes later they were settled in the living room. Samuel sat on the sofa beside Georgia, Ruth in a chair flanking the sofa. Dev remained standing near one of the windows—apart, as if distancing himself from the rest of them.

Georgia looked at him. She didn't want to change things with his family. But she knew he'd see her as a threat to the stability he and his parents had enjoyed since Samuel married Ruth all those years ago.

"I wasn't sure you'd want to acknowledge me," Georgia said, looking at her father. She wanted to ask him why he'd had no contact with his daughters, but didn't want to aggravate the tenuous situation.

"Honey, I didn't even know about you. I could kill your mother. She should have told me."

Georgia looked at him oddly. "My mother has been dead for twenty-two years. I was six weeks old when she died."

"What?" Samuel exclaimed.

"You're only twenty-two?" Dev said.

"We didn't know she'd died," Ruth said with a quelling glance at her son. "Maybe you should explain things to her, Samuel, let her know what happened. I'm sure Georgia has a million questions. We can ask her ours when we've answered hers."

"We know some of what happened," Georgia said. "My grandmother died earlier this year—in February. She was ill for several weeks before her death and Margot cared for her. Something she said made Margot suspicious. She and Rand found out you'd been falsely accused of a crime and threatened with prison. That's why you left, right?"

"A murder charge. Thanks to Harriet, Amanda and I had been having trouble in our marriage—ever since we settled at Beaufort Hall. The threat of a trial and prison was more than she could take. I couldn't convince her the charges were false. We had a fight and I left."

He shook his head. "I always thought it was temporary. Tempers were high. And your grandmother was a strong opponent. I didn't know how to fight her. She had money, a name, influential friends. And her daughter's love."

Samuel looked at Ruth. She smiled encouragingly.

"I received a letter from Amanda saying she wanted a divorce, and planned to ask for full custody of our daughters. I only knew about Margot and Shelby."

"So she knew where to find you?" Georgia asked.

"She knew. She wrote several times. The last letter told me she was marrying somebody there in Natchez once our divorce was final. She asked me to never contact her again."

"Not even to see your daughters?"

"I've thought a lot over the years that I should have fought harder. But at the time I was out of work, had no money, no way to fight your grandmother. She had threatened to provide proof that I had killed a man. I would have stood no chance in Natchez against her. When I got Amanda's last letter, I gave up. I had started working the rigs in the Gulf. The pay was great, but there was no way I could do that and have two little girls stay with me—even occasionally. Besides, I know what it's like to be dragged back and forth between warring parents. I didn't want that for my daughters. Amanda assured me the girls would be better off having one father, the man she was marrying."

"She never married anyone else. Never, as far as we can ascertain, even looked at another man. And she died so soon after I was born, she didn't have a chance to do much of anything," Georgia said slowly.

"I didn't even know she was dead," he said. "All these years…"

"Someone must have told you. Why would you have married Ruth?"

"I got a letter a year after I left from Judge

Hargraves. He said I was free to marry again, then proceeded to warn me to stay away from Natchez and Mississippi. I always figured it was guilty conscience on his part. He'd backed Harriet Beaufort when she threatened my arrest.''

Georgia felt overwhelmed. Her grandmother was responsible for much more than just separating her daughter from her husband.

"But Margot and Shelby must have known I cared. I sent cards every year at Christmas and their birthdays. I had to send them to Beaufort Hall since I didn't have Amanda's new address. To this day I've never set foot in Mississippi. But I invited both Margot and then Shelby to visit me when they each turned eighteen. When they didn't respond, I thought Amanda had been correct, they were better without me in their life.''

"They never got any cards," Georgia said slowly. That she knew for a fact. "Harriet must have intercepted them.''

"All these years, lost," Samuel murmured. "Because of pride."

"Pride?"

"I wanted Amanda to come to me on my terms. Wanted her to prove to me that our love was stronger than the ties to her mother. She had to know I would never murder anyone. I stayed away when I should have confronted them all.''

"My sisters and I have speculated that she would have left her mother and gone after you, but that last pregnancy was hard and then she died so soon afterwards," Georgia said gently.

"Amanda's letters?" Ruth asked.

Georgia shook her head. "I can only guess they came from Harriet Beaufort. What's a forged letter or two after everything else she'd done. And it was another example of pride. She wanted a prestigious alliance for Amanda, and refused to let anything stand in her way. Except my mother's death. If it makes you feel any better, she tried the same thing with Margot and her marriage."

"Tell me all about Margot and Shelby, and you. We have a lifetime to catch up on," Samuel said eagerly, clasping her hand in both of his.

"If you will excuse me, I'll head for home. I don't need to hear anything more. I have work to do, and a full day at the office tomorrow," Dev said, pushing away.

Samuel looked up. "Stay a while longer, son. I need to explain to you why your mother and I never mentioned my first marriage. We—"

"I don't need an explanation. It's obviously something you didn't want to talk about." He headed for the door.

"Dev, wait!" Samuel rose and followed his son into the foyer. With a hasty word to Ruth, Georgia followed right behind them.

"This changes nothing between us, Dev. You're still my son," Samuel was saying when she reached the foyer.

For a long moment Dev held his gaze, then nodded once, briefly.

"If you say so."

"You are my son in every way that counts, the only child I helped to raise. I've always been proud of you. I'll always love you. This does not affect our relationship.''

''Thanks, Dad.''

''Dev, wait,'' Georgia said.

''We have nothing to talk about,'' he said. With a quick expressionless glance at her, he was gone.

''Dev!''

CHAPTER TEN

SHE stared at the closed door in disbelief for a long moment before meeting the sympathetic gaze in her father's eyes.

"Let him go, honey. He'll be back. This has been as big a shock to him as it has to me. Give him some time to get used to things. Come and tell me all about you and your sisters."

Georgia longed to run after Dev. They had resolved nothing. She knew he was angry. Would he even listen to her? Would it be better to talk to him later, when he had time to cool down, or now, before he could build barriers and find a reason to avoid ever seeing her again?

This should be one of the happiest days of her life. She'd just found her father!

But somehow the excitement she'd anticipated had dimmed. She longed for Dev. She wanted to explain, make sure he understood. Make sure he could forgive her. Would he ever kiss her again? Repeat his request to become lovers?

"Dev will come around," Samuel said. "Now, tell me everything, leave nothing out! Ruth, do you want to stay up with us?"

"I wouldn't miss this for the world!" she said, her smile warm and full of love.

Hoping he knew his stepson well, that Dev *would* come around, Georgia sat back on the sofa and began

171

to tell her father about growing up in Natchez, the fun she and Margot and Shelby shared, the disappointments. But she kept back the emotions that resulted from never knowing their father. Tonight should be happy, not a time for recriminations and regrets.

She could hardly wait to learn more about what Samuel had done over the years. And then call her sisters.

Early the next morning, Georgia called Shelby.

"It's him!" she said simply.

"What—your Sam Williams is our father?" Shelby exclaimed. "How did you find out? Does he know who you are? Did he ask after me and Margot? How is he? What does he look like? Do you like him? Does he want to see us? I can't believe we found him! It's actually him? How did you do it?"

"Yes, it's him. And I didn't precisely do it. Dev forced the issue." For a moment the pain of his rejection rose and threatened her newfound happiness. She still had to speak with him, clear the air. See where she stood—if anywhere. But first she needed to take care of family business.

"Dev? How did that happen?"

"He saw my name on my driver's license and threatened to call the police. He thought I was trying some scam to get money out of the family. But I insisted he ask his father if he had ever known Amanda Beaufort. I think Dev was more surprised than I was when Samuel said our mother had been his first wife." Georgia paused a moment, trying to catch her breath. It still seemed surreal.

"He was glad to see me, Shelby. Samuel. That's what they call him now, not Sam. And he wrote to you and Margot for years. He even invited you both to visit when you each turned eighteen. The worst was he didn't know our mother had died."

Shelby demanded details and Georgia spent over an hour recounting everything she could remember from the previous evening. Except for Dev's reaction. His leaving without a word. That still hurt, and was too personal to share even with her sister.

When she wound down, Shelby said, "You haven't said anything about his stepson. How is he taking it? Is he bent out of shape to find he's not an only child anymore?"

Trust Shelby to pick up on that omission.

Georgia swallowed, blinking against the threat of tears. "He was mad. At me. And at his parents. They'd never told him about us. I suspect he's also hurt. Samuel trusts him enough to leave his company in his hands, raised him as a father, but never told him about his first wife and family."

"Why not?"

"I asked him that. He said Dev was too young at the time he married Ruth. And when Margot and you didn't take him up on his invitation to visit, he thought it best to just let the past rest. My turning up was quite a shock. A happy one, he keeps telling me."

"What's he like?"

"You'll see for yourself soon. I'm returning home in a couple of days. Samuel and Ruth are planning to come to New Orleans next week. We figured I could go with you to break the news to Margot, and then she'll be prepared when she meets them.''

"Wow, I'm still in shock," Shelby said.

"Yeah, me too. Go tell Patrick and then Rand. But don't any of you dare tell Margot until I get there!"

Georgia hung up and glanced around. Another day or two to visit, to try to bridge twenty-two years apart, then she'd truly have to return home. She had a job to get back to. And nothing holding her in Houston.

Samuel and Ruth had urged her to move into a guest room, but she'd asked to remain in the apartment over the garage. If Dev came looking for her, she wanted privacy. And it would just be for another couple of days. She couldn't wait to see Margot's face when she told her.

By Thursday morning, Georgia knew Dev was not coming. She'd waited impatiently each day, hoping he'd call, or stop by. She delayed her return home twice.

Samuel went into the office for a few hours every morning. He'd mention Dev at dinner each evening, reassuring Ruth Dev would come around soon. And then he'd turn and question Georgia. He was still catching up on every aspect of her life.

Nothing was ever said about the strained relations between Georgia and Dev. But then neither Samuel nor Ruth had known the extent of their interaction.

Both Samuel and Ruth urged her to consider staying with them indefinitely. She could obtain a job as a nurse at one of the local hospitals and live with them. "Give me a chance to get to know my youngest daughter," Samuel had said.

She was happy to share her past, and learn more about her father. But moving to Houston was more than she cared to consider at this time. Her family and her friends were in New Orleans. Everyone who meant anything to her.

Except for Dev.

Each day stretched out endlessly without a word from him. How awkward things would be if she truly considered accepting her father's invitation.

It was better to return home. The sooner she resumed her normal routine, the sooner she would get over Dev.

She shivered. That made the future seem awfully bleak.

"We'll see about that!" she said, jumping to her feet. It had been four days. Tomorrow she was leaving. She had her plane tickets and her bags packed.

But Georgia was not going home without seeing Dev first! He would listen to what she had to say and if she meant anything to him, he'd have to understand.

She dressed with care, donning the suit she'd worn when she first arrived in Houston, when she thought things would be so easy—walk inside the office, ask to see Sam Williams and figure out if he was her father or not. It felt like a lifetime ago.

As she backed her rental car from the driveway, she let her gaze wander over the yard. She hadn't killed everything. At least that was a plus. But she knew with proper care, the place would be a showplace.

When she reached the tower that housed Samuel and Dev's offices, she took the elevator to the top floor. Before she spoke to Dev, she wanted to see her father's office. He wasn't expecting her, but seemed delighted when his secretary ushered her in.

"Come to see where your dad works?" he asked, proudly introducing her to his secretary.

She nodded, smiling brightly. "I didn't get any trips here as a youngster. Don't kids usually visit where their parents work? Wow, this is great." The office was spacious, with windows on two walls.

"I'd probably never get anything done with a view like this," she said walking over to one of the windows. She felt shaky inside. Was she really interested in seeing this office or was it a stalling technique to put off her visit to Dev's?

"Want me to show you around?" Samuel asked, coming to stand beside her.

"No, thanks. I just wanted to see where you work. I'm on my way to talk to Dev before I head for home."

Samuel rubbed his chin, shook his head. "The boy's riding a grudge, honey. Damn, Ruth and I did what we thought best under the circumstances. You'd think he could see that."

Georgia smiled sadly at her father's soft Texas drawl and choice of words. "He's hardly a boy."

Samuel nodded. "I know. But I often think back to when Dev was a tough defensive young kid longing for happiness and so afraid to trust anyone."

"And Elizabeth did nothing to strengthen his concept of trust. Or me. But I still want to tell him goodbye."

"Don't go, honey. You know Ruth and I would love to have you stay with us."

"I know," Georgia said smiling warmly at her father. "And I appreciate the offer. But my home is in New Orleans. Besides, I can't wait to tell Margot. She remembers you, you know. She'll be so thrilled."

"You'll have to come visit often. You and your sisters. And I'll have to meet their husbands, see that cute Mollie you're always talking about."

She nodded. They'd discussed this a million times since Sunday night. But she thought it gave her father pleasure to speak of his daughters, to imagine becoming a part of their lives after all the years apart.

"I might just visit every couple of months." And wouldn't Dev love that!

Two minutes later she opened the door to Dev's office. Samuel had overridden his secretary's objections to Georgia's slipping in unannounced.

He sat at his computer screen, staring at a spreadsheet of numbers. Georgia's heart caught. He looked tired. Had he been having trouble sleeping at night? She sure had.

"Hi, Dev," she said softly.

He spun around. For a moment she thought he would stand, but he relaxed and leaned back in his chair, watching her warily.

"What are you doing here?"

"I came to see you."

"Why? I think we said all we had to say a few nights ago."

She leaned against the door. His office wasn't as large as his father's, but he still seemed a million miles away.

"I'm sorry for the deception. At first I didn't think it would matter. I was harming no one, and really wanted to find out if Samuel was my father. But as we became friends—''

"Friends? Is that what you call it?" he interrupted.

"I thought we were friends. Or becoming friends." If she had said yes, they could have become lovers.

"I don't need your type of friendship. You got what you want, why bother me anymore?"

"I don't mean to bother you, I just came to say goodbye."

He went still. "Goodbye?"

"I'm leaving. Since you seem to be avoiding your parents while I'm there, I didn't think you'd be dropping by their home any time soon. So I came here to say goodbye."

Slowly he stood, still watching her closely.

"And where are you going? Home to pack up?"

She shook her head. Pushing away from the door, she walked to the window. He shared some of his father's view. Hoping she looked casual and at ease, she glanced at him over her shoulder.

"I'm returning to New Orleans. I have a new job starting soon. And I want to be the one to tell my sister Margot about our father."

He stepped around the desk, almost crowding her when he stopped. "What game are you playing now? I know Dad asked you to move in with him and Mom."

"And do you begrudge me a chance to get to know my father? It wasn't my fault or his that we don't know one another. You've had him for a long time. A few days isn't too much to ask, is it?"

"Not if it gets you all you want."

She smiled and nodded, swallowing hard against the tears that threatened.

"It did. I have a father who didn't voluntarily abandon me. Who even seems to like me. And your mother is a darling woman. She's so delighted in his happiness. I can't wait for them to meet Shelby and Margot. I'm just sorry you and I have to part this way. I never meant to hurt you."

"A man has to care before he can be hurt."

She nodded again, staring out the window, hoping to hold off the tears. He hadn't cared, he'd made that plain.

"Anyway, I'm sorry for the deception. But, I'd do it again, to find my father."

"The end justifies the means, no matter what? So you use me to get your own way, then say sorry and move on?"

"I didn't expect to fall in love!" she said, almost shouting as she turned to face him. "Which was dumb on my part, right? You told me from the very first you were not interested. This time tomorrow, I'll be gone and your life will resume its normal course. You can see your folks and do whatever you want. I won't *bother* you again. It won't be too hard to come up with reasons to stay away from Houston. And Samuel can see all three of his daughters by coming to New Orleans."

"If you play your cards right, I'm sure Samuel would keep open his offer to let you stay at the house. Wouldn't you like a bit of the glamour of being Samuel Williams' daughter? You could go to parties like the Titans put on, buy designer clothes, take exotic vacations. Money is no object."

Incensed, Georgia clenched her hands into fists.

"You don't get it, do you? It was never about the *money.* It was about *family.* But if you can't see that, if you can't trust your father and mother and even yourself, then there's no explaining things to you. You know what? You remind me of my grandmother. She only saw things as they related to money, old family names, and prestige. Nothing else mattered. I'd be careful of that kind of thinking, if I were you. It can leave you alone and bitter in your old age."

Georgia turned and headed for the door. This meeting had been a mistake. There was nothing left for them to say.

Dev beat her to the door, and held it closed with one hand. Looming over her, he looked down into her blue eyes.

"What can you do to prove me wrong?"

She studied him. Why was he asking? What *could* she do to prove him wrong?

Slowly she released her grip on the doorknob.

"Only time will prove that, Dev. I can promise I'll never tell another lie. But you'd have to know me for a lifetime to see if I keep that promise. I can tell you I love you and would never do anything to hurt you, but again, it would take a lifetime to prove it. You want everything wrapped up in guarantees from the get-go. Life isn't that way. Sometimes you just make a blind leap of faith, hold on and trust that everything will turn out the way you want."

"Are you suggesting *I* should make a blind leap of faith and trust *you* for a lifetime?"

She nodded. "I'd trust you with everything I have. You can trust me, too."

"I want to let you walk out of this office. I want to show you that you can't waltz into a man's life and turn it upside down and get away with it. I want to be strong enough to stand up to your leaving. And be able to tell myself years down the road that my life was better because of it."

He brushed her cheek with the back of his fingers.

"But I can't. These last few days have been hell. One minute I'm so angry with you I can hardly stand it. Then I remember your wide-eyed innocent look, how you delight in listening to my childhood memories, how you can make me forget the rest of the world with just a brush of your hand, or a sudden smile—and I think only of you. Of the laughter that lurks in your eyes, the soft feel of your skin, the sensations of coming home that I get whenever I'm with you."

"Oh, Dev," Georgia whispered, almost afraid to breathe.

"The thought of you flying back to New Orleans and my not seeing you again is more than I wish to live with. So maybe I'll have to take you up on that lifetime of observations. I'll just make sure not to give you cause to lie, and see if I can trust you as much as you trust me."

"I'll sign a prenuptial agreement and everything," she said quickly. "I don't want any of your money. I make enough as a nurse to support myself and will pay my share of the household."

Dev laughed, picked her up and spun her around and around. "Maybe you make enough now, but when the babies come? Don't you want to stay home and watch them grow? Then where would you get money? I think maybe part of my trust has to start with commitment without a prenup. I love you, Georgia Brown Beaufort. I want you to marry me and have my babies. Just think, we'll be one couple who never has in-law problems! Want to give it a try? Want to let me verify that you'll never lie, that you'll always love me? Because I know I love you, and always will.''

"Yes, please," she said as he slowly lowered her to the floor and drew her into his arms.

His kiss was pure bliss. Georgia had come home, too.

November

"Don't get tangled in the veil," Shelby warned Mollie.

"I'm not, I want to see Auntie Georgia all around," Mollie said carefully watching where she put her feet. She beamed up at Georgia.

"You looks pretty, Auntie Georgia," she said.

"You do look lovely," Margot said, sitting on one of the chairs.

Georgia inclined her head regally. "Thank you," she said, gazing into the full-length mirror while Shelby straightened her veil. She smiled dreamily.

"Hasn't this been a wonderful year? Three brides in a row. I can't believe it."

Mollie went to lean against Margot and patted her rounded stomach. "My mommy is gonna have a baby, too, like you, Auntie Margot. Then I'll have a sister or brother to play with."

"What?" Georgia spun around.

Margot sat up and stared at Shelby, her smile wide and delighted.

"Oh, Mollie, sweetie, that was supposed to be a secret," Shelby said, laughing. She looked at Georgia apologetically. "I didn't want to take anything away from your big day. We were going to tell you after the honeymoon."

"Oh, Shelby, how wonderful!" She hugged her sister. "That takes nothing away, for heaven's sakes, it just adds to my happiness. Wow, I'm going to be an aunt three times over! Wouldn't you know it, just when I'm moving away, too."

"Congratulations, Shelby. I'm so happy for you. And Georgia, Houston isn't that far," Margot said, struggling to get up from the chair.

"Are you sure you're all right?" Georgia asked when Margot joined her sisters. The three looked at each other in the mirror. Georgia had insisted on a traditional wedding, with formal gowns, attendants and a church ceremony. She only planned to marry once and wanted it to be a never-forgotten event.

"I'm fine. In a minute Dad will knock and it'll be time for us to go," Margot said, massaging her lower back.

"Dad," Georgia said with a smile. "That's another miracle of the year. I'll forever be sorry he wasn't around while we were growing up, but he's sure made certain he is an active part of our lives now."

"He and Ruth are wonderful."

"And Dev," Georgia said.

Margot and Shelby laughed and exchanged glances. "Yes, Dev is wonderful—and you better keep thinking that."

"I will. All my life," she vowed.

When the knock came on the door, Mollie opened it and reached up her arms. Samuel and Ruth had instantly taken to the little girl, declaring they were pleased as punch to have a ready-made grand-daughter. The first of many, they hoped. Samuel leaned over to pick her up, and smiled at the picture his three daughters made.

"I wish your mother could see you three today. You are all so beautiful. She would have been proud of what you've done with your lives."

"Thanks, Dad." Margot crossed the room and reached up to kiss his cheek. "I don't want to rush anything, but is it time to start?"

"Can't wait for me to tie the knot?" Georgia teased as she followed, kissing Sam on his other cheek.

"Remember how Margot has always mothered us?" Shelby asked, following suit, then relieving him of Mollie. "I think she just wants to know you're safely on your way."

Georgia nodded. "I'm very ready. Can you believe we pulled this off in under three months?"

Shelby set Mollie on her feet, handing her the basket of flower petals. "I believe it. I've spent every free moment on the phone following up on things."

The sound of the church organ could be heard as Margot followed behind Shelby. "All happiness, sis."

Georgia linked arms with her father, smiling up at him.

"This makes the day perfect. Thank you for walking me down the aisle," she said softly.

"It hasn't come any time too soon, you know," he said softly as they moved into place at the end of the aisle. "Dev has about driven us crazy with missing you. At least things can settle down once you two are married and living together in Houston. And I'll have one of my babies close at hand."

The music swelled as they started down the aisle. Georgia smiled at her friends gathered on either side, and then let her gaze rest on Dev. Her heart skipped a beat, then began to race. Her hands grew damp, and her breathing became difficult. He was as gorgeous as the first time she saw him. And her heart almost burst with happiness and love. She knew over the recent months things had been settled between them. Her love grew each day. She trusted his did as well. Now their life together began.

Dev watched, giving nothing away with his expression as her father escorted her down the aisle. Ruth sat in the front row of the groom's side. Samuel was planning to sit with Rand and Patrick on the front row of the bride's side.

But Georgia didn't care about any of it now. She had eyes only for Dev. When her father handed her to him, her happiness was complete.

"Dearly beloved," began the minister.

Dev leaned close. "That's you, Georgia, you are my dearly beloved."

With those words, she knew he'd finally, fully forgiven her deception. Life was wonderful.

EPILOGUE

THE nurse behind the counter looked up, widening her eyes at the sight of an entire wedding party descending on her.

"We're here to see Margot Marstall," Shelby said.

"And baby," Patrick added.

"We were told visiting hours started at seven."

"Yes," said the nurse, the puzzlement obvious in her eyes. "She and the baby are in room 234. Usually we limit the number of visitors—"

"She'll want to see us, we're all her family."

"And I'm the baby's cousin," Mollie said from her perch in her father's arms.

"We would have come right away when she was admitted, but we had the reception to see to," Ruth explained. "We couldn't dash out and leave all the guests."

"She was already in the beginning stages of labor during the ceremony, but didn't want to take the limelight away from us," Georgia said. "She was my matron of honor."

"Oh, well, go right down the hall, it's the fourth door on the left," the nurse said, obviously not clear on the situation despite the hurried explanations.

Everyone crowded into Margot's room. Georgia and Dev hugged her, then Shelby and Patrick and Mollie. When Sam drew her into his arms, she began to cry. Rand held her hand and handed her a hand-kerchief. Ruth gave her a quick kiss.

"I want to see my grandson," Samuel said, peering into the bassinet beside the bed.

Rand lifted the tiny infant, holding him with confidence. "John Samuel Marstall, meet your grandfather."

Samuel's eyes grew suspiciously moist as he gazed around the gathering of his family. "I never expected this day. I am truly blessed."

Margot, Shelby and Georgia smiled. "Welcome to the family, Dad," they said in unison.

Harlequin Romance®

Experience the ultimate desert fantasy with this thrilling new Sheikh miniseries!

Four best-loved Harlequin Romance® authors bring you strong, proud Arabian men, exotic eastern settings and plenty of tender passion under the hot desert sun....

Look out for:

His Desert Rose by Liz Fielding
(#3618) in August 2000

To Marry a Sheikh by Day Leclaire
(#3623) in October 2000

The Sheikh's Bride by Sophie Weston
(#3630) in November 2000

The Sheikh's Reward by Lucy Gordon
(#3634) in December 2000

Available in August, September, October and November wherever Harlequin Books are sold.

HARLEQUIN®
Makes any time special.™

Visit us at www.eHarlequin.com   HRSHEIK2

**Don't miss
an exciting opportunity
to save on the purchase of
Harlequin and *Silhouette* books!**

Buy any two Harlequin or
Silhouette books and save
$10.00 off future Harlequin
and Silhouette purchases

OR

buy any three
Harlequin or Silhouette books
and save **$20.00 off** future
Harlequin and Silhouette purchases.

**Watch for details
coming in October 2000!**

PHQ400

HARLEQUIN®
Makes any time special ™

Silhouette®
Where love comes alive ™

If you enjoyed what you just read,
then we've got an offer you can't resist!

Take 2 bestselling love stories FREE!

Plus get a FREE surprise gift!

Clip this page and mail it to Harlequin Reader Service®

IN U.S.A.	IN CANADA
3010 Walden Ave.	P.O. Box 609
P.O. Box 1867	Fort Erie, Ontario
Buffalo, N.Y. 14240-1867	L2A 5X3

YES! Please send me 2 free Harlequin Romance® novels and my free surprise gift. Then send me 6 brand-new novels every month, which I will receive months before they're available in stores. In the U.S.A., bill me at the bargain price of $2.90 plus 25¢ delivery per book and applicable sales tax, if any*. In Canada, bill me at the bargain price of $3.34 plus 25¢ delivery per book and applicable taxes**. That's the complete price and a savings of 10% off the cover prices—what a great deal! I understand that accepting the 2 free books and gift places me under no obligation ever to buy any books. I can always return a shipment and cancel at any time. Even if I never buy another book from Harlequin, the 2 free books and gift are mine to keep forever. So why not take us up on our invitation. You'll be glad you did!

186 HEN C4GY
386 HEN C4GZ

Name	(PLEASE PRINT)	
Address	Apt.#	
City	State/Prov.	Zip/Postal Code

* Terms and prices subject to change without notice. Sales tax applicable in N.Y.
** Canadian residents will be charged applicable provincial taxes and GST.
   All orders subject to approval. Offer limited to one per household.
   ® are registered trademarks of Harlequin Enterprises Limited.

HROM00_R2   ©1998 Harlequin Enterprises Limited

Romance is just one click away!

online book **serials**

➤ *Exclusive* to our web site, get caught up in both the daily and weekly online installments of new romance stories.

➤ Try the Writing Round Robin. Contribute a chapter to a story created by our members. Plus, winners will get prizes.

romantic **travel**

➤ Want to know where the best place to kiss in New York City is, or which restaurant in Los Angeles is the most romantic? Check out our Romantic Hot Spots for the scoop.

➤ Share your travel tips and stories with us on the romantic travel message boards.

romantic reading **library**

➤ Relax as you read our collection of Romantic Poetry.

➤ Take a peek at the Top 10 Most Romantic Lines!

Visit us online at

www.eHarlequin.com
on Women.com Networks

HEUT1

Coming in October 2000

HARLEQUIN®
AMERICAN ◆ ROMANCE®

brings you national bestselling author

ANNE STUART

with her dramatic new story...

A man untamed, locked in silence.
A woman finally ready to break free.

$4.25 U.S.
$4.99 CAN.
October

HARLEQUIN®
AMERICAN ◆ ROMANCE®

WILD THING

ANNE STUART

"The incomparable Anne Stuart delivers romance, passion and adventure in this exciting tale. Don't miss it!"
—Susan Wiggs, national bestselling author

Available at your favorite retail outlet.

HARLEQUIN®
Makes any time special ™

Visit us at www.eHarlequin.com.

HARWT